Fay's brown eyes sparkled with fun.

'You wouldn't deny a poor, overworked midwife her evening off, Dr Grant?' Fay pleaded in a piteous tone.

'I suppose not, but mind how you go, Sister Fay,' he warned, looking down indulgently as if she were a girl of about twelve.

'I surely will, kind sir, when you decide to let me go,' she answered demurely, and Lewis realised that he was still lightly holding her shoulders.

Dear Reader

Babies loom large this month! Lilian Darcy takes us to the Barossa Valley vineyards in Australia and an obstetric practice, while Margaret Holt's second book takes us back to the midwifery unit at Beltonshaw Hospital. Two aspects of general practice are dealt with by Laura MacDonald and Janet Ferguson, though single doctor practices must be rare now! Hope you like them. . .

The Editor

Margaret Holt trained as a nurse and midwife in Surrey, and has practised midwifery for thirty-five years. She moved to Manchester when she married, and has two graduate daughters. Now widowed, she enjoys writing, reading, gardening and supporting her church.

Margaret believes strongly in smooth and close co-operation between the obstetrician and the midwife for safe care of mothers and their babies.

Recent title by the same author:

A PLACE OF REFUGE

A MIDWIFE'S CHOICE

BY

MARGARET HOLT

MILLS & BOON LIMITED
ETON HOUSE   18–24 PARADISE ROAD
RICHMOND   SURREY   TW9 1SR

For Wendy, Margaret and Susan,
Elizabeth and Rosalind,
In loving memory of their Daddy,
ALLAN MARSTON HOLT.

*First published in Great Britain 1992
by Mills & Boon Limited*

© Margaret Holt 1992

*Australian copyright 1992
Philippine copyright 1992
This edition 1992*

ISBN 0 263 77846 0

*Set in 10 on 11½ pt Linotron Times
03-9209-55986*

*Typeset in Great Britain by Centracet, Cambridge
Made and printed in Great Britain*

CHAPTER ONE

'OH, MY God! I can't stand these pains much longer, Sister!' gasped Mrs Irene Forbes, in labour with her first child. She frantically gripped the bed-rail above her head while her husband grasped her other hand, to which an intravenous drip was attached.

Young Sister Fay Mitchell bit her lip. Where on earth was the anaesthetist? Mrs Forbes had requested an epidural twenty minutes ago, and both she and her husband were reaching the limits of their patience.

'Look, Irene, I know that your contractions *seem* to be unbearable,' she said soothingly, 'but you're making very good progress, your baby's heartbeat is fine, and if you could only try to relax a little between the pains——'

'It's sheer *hell*!' Irene screamed as another contraction began, and Mr Forbes's anxiety overcame his self-control.

'I intend to complain to the health authority about this disgraceful delay!' he exploded. 'My wife has been lying here in agony for hours, and we were distinctly told at the parentcraft session that an epidural anaesthetic would be available on request!'

'Please keep calm,' ordered Fay quietly. 'The anaesthetist is in the accident and emergency department, and will be here just as soon as he possibly can.'

She was about to pick up the wall telephone to ask the switchboard to bleep the anaesthetist again, when the door opened and there at last stood Dr Lewis Grant, a man of middle height and deceptively strong

5

build, though his sharply defined features and sensitive mouth made him appear more intellectual than athletic; he gave an impression of being older than his thirty-six years.

'Good morning,' he smiled, and his tired grey eyes lit up at the sight of Fay, even though she muttered,

'And about time, too!' out of the corner of her mouth as he entered the room.

'Irene, this is Dr Grant, anaesthetic registrar,' she said aloud, 'and this is Mrs Forbes who is having her first baby and would like an epidural. Cervix three centimetres dilated, contractions one in five, blood-pressure one-thirty over eighty,' she added.

'Good. Thank you, Sister. Hello, Mrs Forbes, how are things——?'

'Oh, just get on with your job, man!' interrupted the husband angrily.

Lewis Grant did not reply, but removed his white coat and started scrubbing his hands and forearms at the washbasin while Fay uncovered the epidural trolley and set out his sterile gloves and gown. The presence of the quiet man with his thoughtful grey eyes and unhurried manner had a calming effect on Irene, even before he commenced the procedure. Marvellous what a white coat will do, thought Fay, though she knew that there was more to it than that; she had observed Dr Grant's way with patients, and his settling effect on them. The deeply etched lines on his forehead and silver glints among his crisp dark curls hinted at some sadness in his own life that gave him a special understanding and sympathy.

Irene clung to Fay as another contraction began, but she was no longer panic-stricken. Lewis's cool, gentle fingers probed along her spine, searching out the exact spot where the epidural cannula would pierce through to the space around the spinal cord. He gave a small injection of local anaesthetic before expertly inserting the long, hollow needle through which the fine plastic cannula could be guided in to bathe the nerve centres in blissful relief without loss of consciousness, and without affecting the uterine contractions.

When he had finished, Irene closed her eyes and sighed with thankfulness; although her abdomen was tightening with another strong contraction, she was entirely free from pain.

'That's wonderful, Dr Grant,' she said gratefully. 'I shall be able to co-operate now!'

'Good. Sister Mitchell will top it up for you in about two hours if necessary,' he assured her. 'I'd like a word with *you*, Forbes,' he went on, beckoning the husband out into the corridor. Closing the door, he spoke levelly.

'Husbands like you are probably better in the pub than at the bedside. For heaven's sake get a grip on yourself, or you'll be of no bloody use to your wife when she delivers.'

Leaving Mr Forbes gaping, he walked briskly away while Fay cleared the trolley and re-checked Irene's blood-pressure. A few minutes later she found him in the office, writing up the epidural form.

'What kept you? It seemed like forever,' she said reproachfully.

'Sorry. A little chap sliced the top off his finger with an electric bread-knife, and was brought into A and E just before you bleeped me.'

'Oh, *no!*' Fay shuddered. 'Did you have to anaesthetise him in A and E?'

'Yes, for a preliminary clean-up and dressing before he was admitted to Children's. Mother hysterical, father rushing in from his workplace shouting and swearing—it was no fun.'

'And you were on call last night, weren't you?' she sympathised. 'Can I tempt you to a coffee?'

'Try me, Sister Mitchell!'

He followed her into the ward kitchen where she plugged in the electric kettle. He regarded her petite figure and bright, vivacious expression with an inward sigh as he commented on Mr and Mrs Forbes.

'Just one more couple who were expecting to have a normal, natural, pain-free, doctor-free childbirth, I suppose! Nice people, but she wasn't prepared for the unexpectedly high level of pain.'

A shadow fell across his face as he turned to gaze out of the window at the autumnal sky. Fay stole a glance at his profile, noting the frown lines between his eyes and the tension of his mouth; she wondered what had happened to make him the grave and solitary man he appeared to be.

He suddenly turned and caught her questioning look. Fay was used to admiring glances, but what she now saw in Lewis Grant's eyes was something more. She heard the kettle click itself off, but could not turn away from him. Should she smile, speak and break the spell?

No. She stood quite still as he laid his hands lightly on her shoulders. He's going to kiss me, she thought incredulously. Here, in the kitchen—*Lewis Grant*? Why don't I move away? Why don't I——?

'My dear Sister Mitchell, I beg your pardon for intruding, but is it convenient for me to do a round of my antenatal patients?'

And there at the door stood Mr Horsfield, consultant obstetrician and gynaecologist, immaculate in a tailored tweed suit and observing her with mock severity over the top of his gold-rimmed half-moon spectacles.

He was accompanied by house officer Dr Rose Gillis, who looked frankly amused, and registrar Dr Nicholas Lisle who had a distinctly annoyed expression on his handsome face.

Fay coloured to the roots of her dark, curly hair.

'Certainly, Mr Horsfield—sir,' she replied, snapping to attention, the strange spell broken as Lewis drew away from her.

'I heard that the delivery unit was busy this morning, but *you* don't appear to be particularly pressured, Sister,' remarked the consultant slyly, though his eyes were teasingly tolerant of his favourite midwife. It had been on Mr Horsfield's special recommendation that Fay had obtained the post of midwifery sister at the age of twenty-five, over other applicants with longer experience, and much to the irritation of Miss Clothier, the senior nursing officer for midwifery at Beltonshaw General Hospital. She considered Fay's manners much too pert, and deplored her popularity with the doctors.

'She's too much inclined to voice her own opinions for one so junior, in my view,' Miss Clothier had objected.

'Nonsense! The girl's a breath of fresh air in the place,' Mr Horsfield had insisted. 'I've seen the way that she can always raise a laugh among the long-stay antenatals who can get so depressed and touchy. She has the knack of meeting every patient on her own level, adjusting her manner and way of speaking to match theirs. She *listens* to them, and goes to a lot of trouble to help them over their social problems. Anyway, I want her to be sister in charge of the antenatal ward!'

And Miss Clothier had had to give way, though with a very bad grace. Fay had been in her post for nearly a year, and was much appreciated by the mothers who had to spend varying periods of their pregnancy in hospital. From time to time she lent a hand on the consultant delivery unit, and that was why she had been looking after Mrs Forbes that morning, while the CDU staff had been busy in both delivery-rooms. She quickly explained this to the consultant.

'Ah, yes. The role of the anaesthetist in obstetrics is of increasing importance,' he smiled with a sharp glance at Dr Grant. 'Tell me, Sister Mitchell, dear, is Mr Rowan available to join my ward-round?'

'I believe he's just finished a forceps delivery, sir—I'll go and see if he's free,' answered Fay hastily, disappearing up the corridor and straightening her cap as she went. Whatever must Mr Horsfield think? she asked herself crossly. And what on earth had come over Lewis Grant this morning?

'Do I smell coffee? Perhaps we could have a tray in the office while we're waiting for Rowan,' suggested Mr Horsfield, and as there were no nursing auxiliaries around Lewis deftly set out half a dozen cups and refilled the kettle, while Rose Gillis got out the coffee-jar and a bottle of milk. When Fay returned with Mr Rowan, the senior obstetric registrar, she found the consultant sitting with a cigar in his hand, expansively addressing his team over a clatter of cups on the office desk.

'Did any of you see our illustrious Miss Ann Clothier and her birthing-room on the local TV news, being interviewed by that enormous lady journalist?' he was asking.

Nicholas Lisle stiffened slightly.

'I thought the programme excellent, sir. I'm convinced that Ann Clothier's ideas about natural childbirth are sound, and that the mothers benefit tremendously from her birthing-room here.'

'Ah, yes, you *would* say so, Lisle, seeing that you're going in for private practice. I don't envy you the insurance costs—the BMA won't touch it, you know,' grunted the consultant with an amused gleam in his eye that infuriated Nicholas, though he had enough discretion to conceal the fact.

'I do indeed intend to open a birthing clinic on the lines of Miss Clothier's methods, sir, and I'd better warn you that I may take with me one or two of your best staff from here!' he answered boldly, glancing towards Fay, who blushed crimson for the second time that morning.

Mr Horsfield raised a quizzical eyebrow.

'Really? If any member of staff in this unit accepts your kind invitation, Lisle, I shall wish them luck!' he chortled amiably, filling the office with the aroma of his Havana. Fay was grateful for his unruffled good humour.

'You have to admit, sir, that more and more of your antenatal patients are requesting delivery in the birthing-room,' persisted Nicholas, determined to win the argument, especially in front of Fay. 'Ann Clothier can't actually take any more bookings for October, and only a few for November.'

'Oh, I shouldn't worry about the pressure on Miss Clothier's little boudoir,' replied the consultant with a wink at the others. 'Seeing that about fifty per cent of all the birthing-room bookings get transferred to the consultant delivery unit, either during pregnancy or in labour, there will be plenty of last-minute vacancies! You must blame our friend Grant here! He flatly refuses to give epidurals in the boudoir, so the mothers have to be transferred over to CDU. Isn't that so, Grant?'

'None of the anaesthetists would give an epidural

without an intravenous drip up and continuous foetal monitoring, Mr Horsfield, and well you know it!' answered Lewis with the easy familiarity that rose from mutual respect for each other's expertise.

'Your outlook is somewhat antiquated, surely,' observed Nicholas with a slight sneer at the anaesthetist. 'Have you ever actually *practised* obstetrics?'

He was unprepared for the blazing contempt on Lewis's face as he rose from his chair and spoke in a low, controlled tone to the younger man.

'Let's say I have enough personal experience of obstetrics to be able to swear that any woman *I* cared about would be delivered in a consultant unit where she and her child could be reasonably sure of safety—OK?'

Fay felt his scorching gaze rest briefly upon herself as he briskly took his leave.

And she wondered why a pleasurable little shiver ran down her spine. . .

CHAPTER TWO

THE golden sunshine of a mellow September had given way to chilly October mists, and a windy spell had shaken the leaves from the trees that lined the avenue from the nurses' home to the main hospital building. The maternity wing which had been built on to the rear of the hospital looked out on to its own garden area where in summer the long-stay antenatal patients could sit outside on the grass and watch the comings and goings between the various outbuildings—the pharmacy, laboratory and the office headquarters of the Beltonshaw Health Authority. This area was now deserted, the lawn was carpeted with fallen yellow leaves, and a mass of bronze chrysanthemums blazed along its inner border, wafting their sharp and pungent fragrance up to the half-open windows of the antenatal ward and consultant delivery unit on the first floor.

Dr Grant sniffed the autumnal scent appreciatively as he approached the entrance to the ground floor of Maternity, where the post-natal ward and nursery were situated between Miss Clothier's birthing-room and the special care baby unit. As he neared the door, it suddenly burst open and out hurtled Sister Fay Mitchell, her scarlet-lined navy cloak over her uniform dress, and her white cap slightly askew on her dark curls.

'Whoops! Are you in *such* a hurry to get off duty, Sister?' he asked, catching her as she charged full-tilt against his white coat. Holding out his arms, he steadied her shoulders as she apologised in confusion. Looking up and seeing his amused expression, however, she quickly relaxed and returned his smile: there was something so reassuring about Lewis Grant.

'You surely wouldn't deny a poor, overworked midwife her evening off, Dr Grant?' she pleaded in a piteous tone, though her brown eyes sparkled with fun.

'I suppose not, but mind how you go, Sister Fay, or you'll fall headlong on these wet leaves,' he warned, looking down indulgently as if she were a girl of about twelve. 'Have a nice evening, my dear, only be careful!'

'I surely will, kind sir, when you decide to let me go,' she answered demurely, and he realised that he was still lightly holding her shoulders. He quickly dropped his hands and stepped back. Fay wrapped her cloak around her, conscious of an odd little chill as she was released from the security of his half-embrace.

'Thank you, Dr Grant! If I'm late for my date, I shall say I was delayed by a rampaging anaesthetist. Dear me, no respectable woman is safe these days, not even in the grounds of a hospital!'

She clucked in mock indignation as she hurried on, and Lewis turned to watch her retreating figure. There was a softness, a yearning tenderness in his look, as if he longed for something that he could never dare to claim. As her neat little outline disappeared round the corner of the building, he sighed to himself and turned to continue on his way past Post-Natal and up the stairs to Antenatal. He had to see a patient who was for elective Caesarean section the following morning. Her first baby was lying in the breech position, and Mr Horsfield took no chances: Dr Grant would give her the sleep of oblivion while registrar Mr Rowan safely extracted the baby from the body that had nourished and protected it for nine months.

*   *   *

Fay skipped up the steps to the front entrance of the nurses' home, and took the lift to the third floor where her room faced an enclosed garden of lawn and flower-bordered pathways. She closed the window, above which an earthenware pot of trailing ivy hung from a hook. Removing her cloak, she took out the white kirby-grips that held her cap in position on her unruly dark curls. Unbuttoning the navy dress with its crisp white piping of the collar and cuffs, she let it slide down her body, then stepped out of it, rescuing the red and black Biro pens and pair of scissors which cascaded out of the top pocket on to the carpet.

Standing in her blue underslip at the wash-basin, she called out a cheerful, '*Avanti*!' in response to a knock at the door. A tall Trinidadian girl dressed in a brilliant embroidered caftan entered the room and sat down gracefully on Fay's bed.

'Shut the door, Susannah—you never know who's prowling the corridors these days,' said Fay, splashing her face and arms. 'I don't trust the boys to keep to their quarters, especially Randy Ron from ITU in his Batman outfit, rehearsing for the Hallowe'en party!'

Susannah Starr smiled tolerantly. At twenty-seven she too was a midwifery sister, at present working on the delivery unit. A quietly attractive black girl of a thoughtful disposition, she and Fay had become firm friends, the gravity of the one and the high spirits of the other finding a mutual attraction.

'I hear that Dr Nicholas Lisle has asked you to be his partner at that party, Fay,' she remarked. 'Are you going to accept?'

'I can't think of any reason why I should refuse,' replied Fay. 'It'll tie me up for the evening, but there's nobody else that I——' She broke off uncertainly.

'He obviously admires you,' smiled Susannah.

'Everybody can see that! Forgive me, Fay, but we all know that he wants you to be his midwife partner in this birthing clinic he's planning to open in Manchester. How do you really feel about that? I mean, about leaving here and going into private practice—it doesn't sound like *you*, somehow.'

'I know, I know,' sighed Fay, shaking her head. 'It's a great temptation, of course, Susannah, and terribly exciting, but—well, I just can't seem to come to a decision about it. Nicholas wants me to get some experience of delivering mothers in the birthing-room here, but of course Miss Clothier wouldn't like *that*, would she? She likes to conduct them all herself, and, besides, she has ideas of her own about becoming the top midwife at his clinic.'

'Really?' asked Susannah in surprise. 'Has he asked her?'

'No, not yet,' answered Fay in some embarrassment.

'But he's asked you?'

'Yes. And I can't decide. Oh, please keep it to yourself, Susannah, love—Miss Clothier would go bananas if she suspected that——'

'Fay, have you ever known me to spread hospital gossip?' asked the Trinidadian girl reproachfully.

'Never! I know I can rely on you, Susannah. Now, let's change the subject. You look as serious as dear old Lewis Grant—and, by the way, I bet he and Matthew Okoje talk things over with each other, just as we do. Those two are great pals, aren't they? Both jolly good anaesthetists, everybody likes them, and—oh, Susannah, you *must* have noticed Matthew's eager glances in your direction!'

Sister Starr bit her lip and looked away.

'You do say some ridiculous things, Fay. Why should Dr Okoje, who is a Ugandan, be interested in a woman of a different nationality, different culture, different faith——?'

'But the same human race, Susannah, and with a very similar nature to his own!' insisted Fay. 'Anyway, I'm just glad that Lewis has got Matthew to exchange opinions and ideas with, otherwise he'd be such a loner, wouldn't he? Haven't you noticed a sort of sadness about Lewis, as if he had some private burden that nobody else knows about? I mean he's so *nice*, and all the patients trust him completely, and the house-surgeons respect him, even though they make wisecracks like, "Lo, the gas-man cometh!" He's never moody, no matter what hour of the day or night he's called, and sometimes on Maternity, when we're having one of those post-delivery discussions over coffee in the office, he relaxes and becomes a completely different man, and——'

Fay suddenly stopped her eager flow of words as she became aware of an amused expression on Susannah's face.

'Oh, no, I don't mean that I—that he——' She laughed at the question in her friend's eyes. 'You're just getting back at me because I teased you about Matthew Okoje, who really *does* worship you from afar! Why don't you make him happy by going with him to the Hallowe'en party? I'm sure he's dying to ask you, but just can't pluck up courage!'

'Honestly, Fay, don't you think seriously about *anything*?' protested Susannah. 'You know I'm no good at parties. And besides, there's a West Indian evening at my church that night, and I'd much rather go to that.'

'Oh, you're such a churchy old thing! Mind you, sometimes I get a little bit suspicious,' grinned Fay. 'Tell me, is there some lucky minister in a dog-collar who's hoping to be favoured, perhaps?' The irrepressible girl turned to look at her friend as she waited for an indignant retort.

But Susannah lowered her proud head in hesitation, saying in a low voice, 'And suppose that I tell you that I *have* met a good man, Fay Mitchell, would you joke about it?'

Fay put her hand over her mouth apologetically.

'Susannah, *dear*!' she exclaimed. 'I didn't mean to be rude, honestly, only I just can't resist teasing you. Oh, sweetie, if there *is* someone at your church, I couldn't be more pleased for you! Tell me more—go on, I won't laugh.'

'I think I'd better not say too much just yet, Fay, because it's not quite—I mean, there are details to be discussed, you see,' murmured Susannah shyly, then stopped as she found herself being kissed and hugged by a delighted Fay.

'Oh, you naughty old dark horse! Why didn't you tell me before? This is wonderful! *Is* he a—a clergyman, then?'

'No, just a very charming gentleman who comes to my church. He came to a wedding in the spring, and has attended regularly ever since. We've got to know each other, and we have gradually become closer. So close, Fay,' she said earnestly, her big, lustrous eyes shining with happiness.

'You'll be making me cry in a minute—with envy!' said Fay with a loving smile. 'What would I give to be as certain as you are! Tell me, when am I allowed to meet this gorgeous hunk?'

'Not for a while. He's away for a few weeks. He's Jamaican, you see, and flew home last week. He has to tell his parents about us, and there'll be an announcement when he gets back. Don't spread it around before then, Fay—you know what this hospital's like for gossip.'

'Guide's honour!' Fay assured her with an authentic salute. 'What's his name?'

'Quentin. He's on the staff of *Coral Strand* magazine, and works in their Manchester office. He's gone to do some up-to-date sketches of the Leeward Islands for the spring edition. He's a very talented artist,' said Susannah with modest pride.

'Well, who'd have thought it? Our Sister Starr! You'll be married and on maternity leave by this time next year, while I'll still be plodding on here as a poor old midwife in a woman's world!' wailed Fay in mock despair.

A strange, almost anxious expression briefly crossed Susannah's face before she replied.

'Oh, nonsense! You and Dr Lisle seem to have a very good working relationship that could lead to a partnership in more ways than one!'

Fay sighed. 'Time will show. Anyway, love, are we still going to see this film at the Canal Studios? What shall I wear? I wish I had a Junoesque figure like yours and could carry off that super caftan! But I'll have to make do with my little black skirt and white blouse, and show off my legs with black lacy tights and strappy shoes!'

The two young women made a striking contrast as they entered the Outsiders, a popular wine bar on Beltonshaw's main road. They planned to have a light meal before going on to the cinema complex overlooking the ship canal, which offered a variety of new films currently on release. Heads turned as they took their places at a corner table with a bench seat on two sides.

'Shall we have a sherry to warm us up?' suggested Fay, taking out her bag.

'No, no,' said Susannah hastily. 'Fruit juice for me.'

'I say, look who's just come in!' came a delighted male voice from the bar. 'What a stroke of luck. Doesn't she look stunning in that black and white outfit? Wow!'

Nicholas Lisle raised his voice to call to the girls, 'Hi! Is this a special party, or can anyone join in?'

He approached their table with his usual self-assurance, and women at other tables turned to look at the well-built, fair-haired man of about thirty, smiling with disarming casualness, seemingly unaware of the impression he was making. His open-necked blue shirt and grey flannels somehow made the suits and ties of other men look dull.

'What are you drinking, ladies? No, I absolutely insist! Gin and tonic? Or a Martini? All right, sherry for you, Fay, darling—sweet or dry? And what about——?' He hesitated, unable to remember Susannah's first name.

'Orange juice, please, Dr Lisle,' requested Susannah with a touch of embarrassment.

'Right you are.' He turned and beckoned to his two companions at the bar. 'Come over here and draw up some chairs while I order, will you?'

Lewis Grant and Matthew Okoje exchanged a quick glance. They had come in together for a quiet drink before Nicholas arrived, and now approached the girls with some hesitation.

'I presume that you are overjoyed at being gate-crashed like this?' smiled Lewis. 'Are you waiting for friends, perhaps?'

'Only you gentlemen, by the looks of things!' Fay assured him, an amused expression on her lively face.

She had noted Lisle's casual attitude towards the other doctors, and his easy assumption that she and Susannah would welcome male company. She also noticed Matthew's shy smile at Susannah as he asked if he might sit down beside her, and the girl's rather strained smile and nod.

'Of course, we're delighted to see you,' Fay went on as Lewis took a seat. 'The only thing is, we're having a little snack here before going on to the Canal Studios, so you'll excuse us if we eat, won't you? Pass me the menu, Susannah. Thanks. I think I'll have lasagne. What about you?'

'I like smoked mackerel. Shall we share a salad?' asked Susannah.

'My dear Fay, we've intruded on your meal in a most unforgivable way!' exclaimed Lewis, though his eyes rested on Fay in undisguised pleasure.

'Not at all. The main film doesn't start until after eight, so we've got an hour to spare yet,' said Fay easily. 'We'll order now, and then enjoy our drinks in your company.'

She spoke with the friendliness of manner that made her popular with patients and colleagues alike, and Lewis looked considerably more relaxed. Nicholas returned from the bar with a tray, and put down five glasses on the table.

'There we are, Fay, your sherry. One orange juice and two lagers,' he announced with a flourish, setting down a whisky for himself.

'Look, Lisle, these girls are having a meal and going on to the cinema,' remonstrated Lewis.

'Great! What are we going to see—Meryl Streep or Mel Gibson?' smiled Nicholas.

'Neither. Susannah and I are going for British comedy,' replied Fay, sipping her sherry.

'*Shirley Valentine* it is, then,' said Nicholas with satisfaction. 'I've got the car outside.'

He had firmly decided that he was not going to miss the chance of Fay's company for the evening. There was a short, awkward silence.

'I should like to see the film,' said Matthew, his smile showing his perfect strong white teeth. 'May I escort you, Miss Starr?'

Fay saw the hesitation on Susannah's face, and felt that Matthew should be told about Quentin without delay.

'You'll have to count me out, I'm afraid,' interposed Lewis. 'I'm taking over Dr Sarangi's calls after eleven, and I must do some reading for my research project.'

'OK, Uncle Lewis,' grinned Nicholas. 'Duty calls and will not be denied!' Grant's withdrawal suited his plans.

The girls' meals were served, and the men ordered sandwiches, after which Lewis took his leave. Fay rose to accompany him to the door, and spoke with rather self-conscious politeness.

'I'm sorry you have to go, Lewis. I'd have liked it if you had been able to come too. It's good to get away from the shop occasionally, isn't it?'

'Yes, Fay, but I feel that you and Susannah have been bulldozed into accepting Lisle's company for the evening,' he replied as they walked out of earshot of the others. 'I know that it suits Matthew, but——'

'Actually, there's something I feel I should mention, Lewis,' she interrupted quickly. 'I shouldn't, because I'll be breaking a confidence, but I must say it—and to you.'

'Go on, Fay, my dear. You can trust me,' he said in a low voice as he looked down at her attentively. She knew that she could indeed trust this man.

'It's Dr Okoje. I wonder if he should be warned that Susannah is already as good as engaged to someone else,' she told him quietly.

'I see.' He sighed. 'Yes, that's a pity for Matthew, as I know he likes her. In fact he likes her a lot. Is she definitely planning to be married fairly soon?'

'It sounds like it. He's some Jamaican artist who goes to her church—probably just to meet her there, I'd guess! Anyway, I wouldn't like to see Matthew hurt, so maybe you could drop him a hint—of course, she may find a chance to tell him herself, perhaps this evening. But he really ought to be told, I think,' she added firmly.

'Yes, I agree,' he replied, and then added unexpectedly, 'Because he might be prepared to put up a fight for her, if I know Matthew Okoje.'

'I can't see her changing her mind. Susannah's very much in love,' Fay confided.

'Poor Matthew,' he said with feeling.

'He'll be able to talk with her this evening,' said Fay, with a backward glance towards the table where the other three sat.

'And you, Sister Mitchell, will also be well attended and admired.'

He gave her a penetrating look, and she lowered her eyes. Quiet Dr Grant never missed a thing, damn him.

'Goodnight, Fay. Enjoy the film.'

'Goodnight, Lewis. I'm sure I shall.'

And then, in front of all the patrons of the Outsiders, he leaned forward and kissed her flushed cheek. That was all, a gentle touch of his lips, soft as a butterfly's wing upon her skin. A friend's kiss, such as Mr Rowan might give her when she visited his wife, who was a midwife friend.

So why did her body respond in the way that it did?

The way her heart seemed to miss a beat, the way she caught her breath for a moment and closed her eyes. . .?

A last smile, and he was gone. She returned to the table, a deliciously tingling sensation on the spot where Lewis's mouth had so briefly rested. It took her a few moments to regain her composure and listen to what Nicholas was saying.

'Fay, my love, I don't want to talk shop in here, but I simply must get you inside the birthing-room and give you a demonstration of the Lisle technique. You'll be completely won over, I know.'

'Maybe, but Miss Clothier doesn't allow any but her special favourites in the boudoir,' replied Fay doubtfully.

'I know, there's a little bit of professional jealousy on her part, isn't there? A pity! Now, when's your day off next week?'

'Wednesday.'

'Great. The old girl's off to London on Tuesday to a meeting of the English National Board or whatever it is she sits on. So stay around on Wednesday, love, and if there's a birthing-room delivery I'll tip you off and you can come in with me. There's a Mrs Clare Warburton due any day now, and if she goes into labour she will be an ideal patient for you. Second baby, shouldn't be any trouble at all.'

'And what is Miss Clothier going to say when she comes back and finds my name all over the case-notes, birth forms and register?' asked Fay uncomfortably, though she was very curious to find out more about the birthing-room, of which there were increasingly glowing reports.

'It'll be too late then, won't it, my love?' he grinned conspiratorially. 'Fingers crossed! Let's hope that Clare will oblige us. She's a nice woman, and had a pretty awful time with her first baby. We'll show her how easy and natural the whole thing can be!'

Fay caught his enthusiasm and smiled in spite of herself.

'Hm. We'll see what happens, then. If Mrs Warburton or another birthing-room booking goes into labour at a reasonable hour next Wednesday, I'll be around on my day off—OK?'

'Fabulous! I can't wait to start our partnership,' he whispered, leaning forward and kissing the tip of her nose. She drew back sharply.

'Heavens, not in here!' she murmured, hoping that Susannah had not noticed.

And then she suddenly thought of Lewis Grant's kiss.

In the cinema the seating arrangements were predictable: Nicholas, Fay, Susannah and Matthew. They all agreed that the film was excellent, though some enjoyed it more than others.

'Poor old Grant,' said Nicholas to Fay during the interval. 'Bit of an oddball, isn't he? Goes to stay with his mother on his weekends off, I've heard. Not natural at his age! Still, each to his own way, I guess.'

Fay made no answer, but wondered why she found Lisle's idle remark offensive. He threw an arm casually around her shoulders as the lights dimmed for the second half of the film; Matthew and Susannah sat together in silence, watching the screen with half their thoughts elsewhere.

CHAPTER THREE

IT WAS Wednesday afternoon. Mrs Clare Warburton's labour was progressing well, and Fay was impressed by the relaxed, informal atmosphere in the birthing-room. Nicholas glanced at her from time to time in complacent satisfaction—with himself, with the trusting Clare, who was trying so hard to co-operate, and with the admiring Mr Bernard Warburton. They were all using first names, and Nicholas joked easily as he sat perched on a high stool.

'We'll soon be in the second stage of labour, folks, and this is when it gets really exciting!' he told them. 'You'll feel a little sensation of pressure, Clare, and then——'

'I think I'm getting another contraction now, actually,' gasped Clare, reaching for her husband's hand. 'Yes, it's quite strong, and getting more—*oh*!' She gritted her teeth.

'OK, Clare, breathe it away, that's right!' smiled Nicholas encouragingly.

'I'd forgotten what the pain is like,' apologised Clare as the contraction subsided.

Fay carefully wiped her forehead with a wet face-cloth, feeling rather awkward as they waited with the delivery trolley and heated cot. This was a strange way to spend her day off, but it seemed a good opportunity to watch Nicholas conduct a normal delivery and learn his special technique; she had got to make a decision about her future career in midwifery, and whether or not to accept Dr Lisle's offer of a partnership. Never-

theless she felt uneasy in this special small room that
Miss Clothier had designed and equipped at her own
expense, and upon which she had stamped her forceful
personality.

The birthing-room, irreverently called the boudoir
by Mr Horsfield, was very different from the stage-one
rooms and delivery-rooms of the consultant delivery
unit upstairs. The floral-patterned wallpaper with
matching curtains gave it a homely touch, as did the
bedside table with its shaded lamp and telephone, the
two small armchairs and the magazine rack. The par-
quet floor with its wipe-clean surface was more attractive than glazed tiles, and there were non-slip rugs that
could be placed where they were needed or pushed out
of the way when a delivery was taking place.

'Well done, Clare—your cervix is fully dilated now,'
announced Nicholas, and Fay wrote in the case-notes
that stage two commenced at 15.00 hours.

'This is so very different from last time, isn't it,
darling?' said Bernard to his wife. 'No impersonal
machinery like drips and that horrible monitor thing
clicking away all the time!'

'And that awful doctor who said that if there was no
progress in the next quarter of an hour he'd put on
forceps and *pull* the child out!' shuddered Clare, thankful for a respite between contractions.

'My wife felt totally helpless, with no control over
what was happening,' Bernard told Nicholas, 'but this
time she's actually participating in the birth of our
baby, and so am I!'

'Oh, my God—oh, my *God*!' cried Clare, her voice
rising in fear as another contraction seized her in its
iron grip.

'Good!' replied Nicholas. 'Take a big breath in, hold
it, head forward and push down—push—push—push!

Smashing! Look here, Bernard, your baby's head is just visible at the height of a contraction, see!'

Bernard Warburton was delighted, though Fay was concerned at the way Clare was trying her best not to cry out loud; her face was distorted in a silent grimace as she wrung her husband's hand.

'Here, Clare, take some gas when the pain comes on,' she said, quickly wheeling the blue and white nitrous oxide cylinder to the bedside. 'Put the mask right over your nose and mouth, like this, and breathe it in and out as hard as you can, right at the beginning of the contraction.'

'Oh, thank you, Sister—that was a little better, I think,' sighed Clare gratefully at the end of the following contraction. 'How much longer will it be now?'

'That's up to you, Clare, to push just as hard as you can to help nature do her work,' smiled Nicholas. 'This is how every mother should have her baby, and this is how my clients will deliver at the Lisle Birthing Clinic!'

'Clare had one of those cruel episiotomies with our first baby,' said Bernard. 'The doctor just picked up these scissors from the trolley, and without asking permission told us that he was going to make a cut to help the baby's head to come through. Didn't he, darling?'

His wife, breathing hard on the gas, was unable to reply.

'You won't have to put up with anything like that here!' Nicholas assured them.

'Did you say it was a forceps delivery last time?' Fay enquired politely.

'No, as soon as he'd made that cut, the baby's head was born quite suddenly,' replied Bernard, and Fay felt fairly sure that the episiotomy had saved the need for a forceps delivery on that previous occasion. She could picture the scene all too clearly, and knew that second and subsequent labours were almost always easier than first ones. She wondered how many first-time mothers would book into the Lisle Clinic.

'Here comes another pain—oh, it's coming, it's coming!' cried Clare, her voice rising to a scream. 'I can't take any more of this!'

Fay stepped forward, and, helping Clare to hold the mask over her face, she whispered, 'Here, love, breathe it in and out, that's the way, there's a brave girl. Don't give up, dear, I'm here to help you.'

She suddenly felt furious with both the doctor and the husband, chatting so knowingly in the presence of the woman's ordeal. The incredible smugness of men! What did *they* know about a woman's fear of pain? And the added burden of showing that fear and letting the side down after all her hopes of a natural, drug-free labour?

I'm a midwife, thought Fay—a *mid-wife*, meaning 'with woman' from ancient times. Well, now I'm with Clare, to help her and support her through this trial like a close and understanding woman friend.

Clare smiled up at her, and began to regain the self-control she needed to use each contraction to the full. Nicholas noted this, and gave Fay a nod of approval.

There was a discreet knock at the door, and Lewis Grant quietly entered the room. His observant grey eyes took in the whole scene at a glance.

'Sorry to interrupt, Dr Lisle,' he said in a low tone. 'I've just commenced an epidural on your patient in Stage-One Room A upstairs, the lady with toxaemia. Blood-pressure needs careful monitoring, and she's for a short second stage. I think she'll reach full dilatation within the hour, and I told Sister Starr I'd let you know—OK?'

'All right. Thanks.' Lisle's tone was offhand, and he did not turn round to look at the anaesthetist.

Lewis smiled questioningly at Fay.

'I thought this was your day off, Sister Mitchell?'

'Well, yes, it is, but I'm having a little out-of-hours experience of the birthing-room,' she replied confusedly, annoyed with herself for reddening and looking embarrassed.

Lewis put his head on one side and pursed his lips slightly.

'I didn't know that you needed any instruction in normal midwifery, Sister; in fact I would expect you to be giving it.'

'Do you mind, Grant? I'm getting ready to deliver my patient, and we don't need an audience, thank you very much!' interposed Nicholas dismissively. 'I'm going to scrub up now, Fay, so have the trolley ready, please.'

Lewis left the room with no further comment, though he raised his eyebrows significantly at Fay before noiselessly closing the door behind him. She found herself wishing that he could stay, though she was unable to explain the reason; once again she was conscious of a feeling of safety in Lewis Grant's presence. And now he had gone.

'I wish that man would remember that he's an anaesthetist *only* in this department, and that we don't need his opinions and predictions about patients in labour,' muttered Nicholas as Fay tied the tapes of his sterile green gown at the back.

'Did you say that doctor is an anaesthetist?' asked Clare with a note of pleading in her voice. 'Is there still time for me to have an epidural, please?'

'Oh, dear me, Clare, it's much too late—you're

going to have a *baby* any minute now!' laughed Nicholas. 'We don't need *him* in here!'

However, the second stage of Clare's labour was unexpectedly slow and tedious. All the encouragement that Fay and Nicholas could give by combined effort was needed, and as the minutes ticked by to three-thirty Fay began to wonder if in fact a normal delivery would be possible; but, after what seemed an interminable wait, Nicholas delivered a large baby boy just after a quarter to four, and handed him straight into his mother's arms, still attached to the umbilical cord.

Bernard kissed his wife as tears sprung to his eyes, and as always Fay was moved by the scene which was always like a miracle. The mother's eyes shone with love as she gazed upon her son, and the pain receded into a blurred memory in the rejoicing over the new life.

'A truly normal, natural birth!' exclaimed Nicholas triumphantly as he cut the cord and handed the baby to Fay for weighing, measuring and labelling of his chubby right wrist and ankle.

'Nine pounds, two ounces!' she announced. 'No wonder he took his time!'

Nicholas was disappointed to find that Clare's delicate skin had torn at the site of the former episiotomy, and so stitches would be needed. Fay was more concerned at the non-appearance of the placenta twenty minutes after the birth. Nicholas tried all the usual methods, gently pulling on the cord, pressing on Clare's tummy and asking her to push hard; he asked Fay to hand the baby to Clare for a first breast-feed to stimulate the uterus to contract: all was to no avail. At half-past four, the placenta remained stubbornly inside.

With beads of perspiration on his forehead, Nicholas decided to have one more try at pulling on the cord.

Suddenly it snapped in half, sending up a shower of drops of blood in a wide semi-circle, spattering the ceiling and wall, the bed, the doctor's face, gown, shoes and floor. It was only a very small amount of blood under pressure, but it alarmed the Warburtons, who were not reassured by the words of the doctor which were uttered before he could stop himself.

'Oh, damn and blast it to hell!'

'My God, what's happened?' asked Bernard in dismay.

'Ssh, it's nothing to worry about,' Fay interposed soothingly. 'This placenta—the afterbirth—has stuck to the wall of the uterus, and doesn't want to come out. It happens every so often, honestly. Dr Lisle, I'll ask switchboard to bleep Dr Grant to come and give Clare a GA.'

'A GA? What's that?' demanded Bernard.

'A general anaesthetic, just a light one, while Dr Lisle removes the placenta from inside,' explained Fay.

'An anaesthetic? Oh, no!' wailed Clare. 'I didn't have to have one last time. Please, I don't want to be put to sleep now that my baby's born!'

Nicholas was biting his tongue to suppress his fury.

'I'd give a lot to keep that po-faced anaesthetist out of this!' he muttered grimly to Fay out of the corner of his mouth.

She sighed as she picked up the telephone and dialled the switchboard. She was very sorry that this tiresome complication had occurred, but was thankful that Clare was in a hospital with all the necessary facilities. What a nuisance a retained placenta is, she thought—an occasional but infuriating anticlimax that takes the sparkle out of the joy of a birth, not serious these days, but rotten luck for Clare.

And of course for Nicholas. Fay had not been

impressed by his unprofessional outburst, but guessed how much he must be regretting it. She smiled at the anxious couple.

'Come on, Clare, don't look so glum! You've got a fine, healthy baby boy, and there are far worse things that can happen than a retained placenta. You're in a place where it can soon be dealt with, and— oh, hello again, Lewis, the very man we need!'

She smiled radiantly as she introduced the anaesthetic registrar to the Warburtons.

'Hi, Clare,' he said, and nodded towards her husband. 'What have we here, then? Ah, a beautiful baby boy—congratulations! Has he got a name yet?'

'We'd thought of Alexander,' replied Clare, relieved and reassured by the easy, unhurried manner of this grave-faced man who could smile so tenderly at her new baby.

'Pity about this, Grant,' muttered Nicholas ungraciously, 'but I'll only need a very light GA to get it out. A single shot of Pentothal will do. Fay, love, will you run upstairs and fetch a couple of ampoules from the theatre?'

'Oh, no,' said Lewis quietly but firmly. 'I shall need to transfer this mother to CDU and put up a drip before we do anything else, so all we need right now is the stretcher trolley.'

'Oh, for God's sake, surely you're capable of giving a short GA in here!' protested Nicholas with a sneer. 'I'm damned sure *I* could!'

Lewis completely ignored this taunt.

'Will you please have the stretcher trolley brought in here, Sister Mitchell, so that we can take this lady upstairs and get this little job done for her?' he requested pleasantly, and Fay was eager to obey.

Within minutes Clare was on the trolley, and they all

proceeded along the corridor to the lifts. They were almost there when a formidable female figure in outdoor clothes materialised in front of them. Fay's heart sank.

'Dr Lisle! Sister Mitchell! What's going on here? Where are you taking Mrs Warburton?'

'Retained placenta, Ann,' murmured Nicholas. 'She's had a splendid normal delivery of a nine-pound-two boy, so we're all feeling very happy,' he added between his teeth.

'Oh, if only I'd stayed here today! I *never* have retained placentas!' exclaimed the furious senior midwife. 'It's too bad! I leave this place for just twenty-four hours, and—what are *you* doing, Sister Mitchell? Shouldn't you be on a day off——?'

'Excuse us, please, we're trying to get to the lift,' interrupted Lewis. 'Would you mind? Thank you!'

Fay avoided Miss Clothier's eye as she pushed the trolley forward. This is all we need, she thought, picturing the scene of retribution that would inevitably ensue in the boss's office when she was called to account for her underhand behaviour. Truth to tell, Fay did in fact feel somewhat guilty about the way she had been persuaded to enter the boudoir as soon as Miss Clothier's back was turned.

The operation turned out to be an unexpectedly difficult evacuation of the uterus; the placenta was abnormally adherent, and a curettage, or scraping, was needed to make sure that all of it was safely removed. A longer anaesthetic was needed than had been foreseen, and the total blood loss amounted to a postpartum haemorrhage. Fay caught Lewis's eye, sharing his unspoken comments: it was definitely not a suitable procedure for the boudoir, where the wallpaper and ceiling would need cleaning after the incident with the umbilical cord—something which happened from time to time, but was not considered good obstetric practice.

Fay's thoughts were uneasy, and not just about Miss Clothier's wrath to come. She wondered how Nicholas would cope with a really grave, life-threatening emergency in his birthing clinic, with no consultant delivery unit under the same roof. What arrangements would there be for transferring his patients to hospital, if the need arose? She felt unsure about his ability to deal with a crisis, and even less sure about her own future career as a midwife working alongside him. She caught Lewis Grant looking at her as if he could read her thoughts, and she momentarily closed her eyes. What exactly did she want out of life?

She sighed. What a day off! She took comfort from the thought that tomorrow she would be back on duty with her antenatal ward patients and their problems to keep her mind fully occupied.

And there was the Hallowe'en party to look forward to. . .

The consultant delivery unit and antenatal ward were quiet at the five p.m. change-over on October the thirty-first, and Fay hoped to get off duty promptly. However, Sister Pardoe seemed inclined to talk for a while after taking the report; she was a pleasant-faced, plain-speaking Scotswoman in her late forties, and the immaculately starched, lace-edged cap on her neat grey head denoted her position as senior midwifery sister on CDU.

'Has Miss Clothier forgiven you yet, Sister?' she enquired. Sister Pardoe had not taken to using first names on duty.

'Uh-uh, I don't think she ever will,' replied Fay with a shrug. 'I understand how she feels, of course. It *was* cheeky of me to attend a delivery in the boudoir without asking her permission. But she would never have agreed, and I wanted to see what it was like, so——'

'So you found out, Sister? Serve you right!' said the Scotswoman with mock severity. The story of the retained placenta had been much discussed, and also Fay's serious reprimand from the senior midwife.

'But Dr Lisle got off fairly lightly, I gather?' went on Sister Pardoe with a little smile.

'Yes, well, Miss Clothier's had a soft spot for *him* ever since he gave up his place in a flourishing general practice to come here and learn about her natural birthing technique,' replied Fay.

'She'll be expecting to be his partner in this fancy clinic of his, I'm thinking.'

'Maybe,' said Fay hesitantly.

'He's made good use of her, Sister, flattering her and getting into her good books while learning all she can teach him. It would no' be right to drop the poor woman in favour of somebody younger after all she's done for him—don't you agree, Sister?'

Fay felt distinctly uncomfortable, especially as the perceptive older midwife was expressing many of her own half-formed thoughts. Jealous and self-opinionated Miss Clothier might be, but there was no doubt that Nicholas had made use of her expertise, yet would have few scruples about discarding her if Fay agreed to become his partner.

'Oh, I don't know, Sister Pardoe,' she confided. 'Let's be honest, she's ten years older than he is, and not the easiest of personalities to fit in with his hand-picked team——'

'Certainly not if that team includes *you*, Sister

Mitchell. Anyway, I mustn't delay you from getting ready for the party. Will our Dr Grant be there?'

'Oh, no, it wouldn't be his scene—besides, he's on call tonight,' replied Fay with a sudden awkwardness which she could not explain. 'We're all going as witches and warlocks, except for Rose Gillis who's going to be the Wicked Queen from the Narnia chronicles. And Ron Baines, that charge nurse from Intensive Therapy, you know—he's going as Batman, so I'll keep out of his way!'

'But you'll have Dr Lisle to look after you, won't you, Sister?' remarked the Scotswoman slyly. She flicked over some case-notes lying on the desk, and then asked abruptly, 'Is Sister Starr going?'

'No, it's not exactly her scene, either. She's got some bun-fight tonight at her church.'

'Do you think she looks well, Sister?'

Fay was alerted by the significant look which accompanied the question, and realised guiltily that her own recent experiences had taken up all her thoughts. She had not really noticed Susannah or spoken seriously with her recently, but now, faced with the direct question, she realised that her friend *had* been looking peaky. Fay assumed that she was missing Quentin, and might even be feeling apprehensive about the shower of congratulations and exclamations that would follow the announcement of her engagement.

'I think Susannah has a lot on her mind, Sister Pardoe,' she hesitated. 'I can't really tell you, because it's still unofficial, but I can assure you there's a good reason for her preoccupied air these days!'

'Indeed, Sister? And how much longer does the lass hope to keep it unofficial, I wonder? This *is* a maternity unit, and we can't be expected not to notice certain things.'

Fay stared blankly, then gave a gasp of shocked surprise.

'No, no, Sister Pardoe, you're quite wrong! She's just missing him so much, that's all—her fiancé, I mean. Oh, there now, I've told you. Susannah's far too innocent——'

'Aye, she is that, Sister Mitchell—and maybe too trusting. By the way, I found this on the floor of the staff cloakroom. Perhaps you'll return it to her?'

She handed Fay a colourful picture postcard of a Jamaican beach. Fay turned it over. It was addressed to Miss S. Starr with a brief message.

Hi! This is the place to be, and how! Sea-bathing, sunbathing, socialising, the lot! Not much time for sketching, but plenty of fun. May stay on till New Year. Save yourself for me.

Love, Quentin.

Fay felt a chill of dismay at the superficiality of the few scrawled lines, but tried to speak lightly.

'Thank you, Sister. She must have dropped it. I'll let her have it back.'

'Let's hope he changes his mind and returns to her soon, otherwise she'll be needing a good friend like yourself. Away with you now and get yourself ready for the party!'

'Yes, I'd better be off now,' replied Fay, remembering that Nicholas had invited her to his room for pre-party drinks. 'Goodnight, Sister Pardoe.'

She dashed over to the nurses' home and went straight to Susannah's room. There was no reply to her knock, and she slid the card under the door. Surely Sister Pardoe had to be mistaken. . .

An hour later Dr Rose Gillis came to Fay's room with her costume in a large plastic bag.

'It's safer to change over here than in the residency!' she giggled nervously, and Fay was only too pleased to have the company of the young junior obstetric house officer. They helped each other to dress, and the results were more than satisfying. Fay's tall witch's hat accentuated the piquant little face beneath it, and the clinging black dress showed off her neat figure to perfection.

'Oh, Rose, you look stunning!' she exclaimed in admiration as they stood in front of the mirror. The bewitching Queen of Narnia wore a silvery dress with a high-collared crimson cloak. A spiked crown encircled her head, and her black hair hung loose from a centre-parting. The transformation from white-coated junior doctor was striking.

'Come with me to Nicholas's room, Rose, and don't leave before I do,' begged Fay with unusual shyness.

'Huh! I shall have a great time if I'm going to play gooseberry all the evening,' grumbled the Wicked Queen.

'No way! In that get-up you'll be carried off by Batman to his lair where he'll make passionate love to you till dawn—hey! Don't throw things at me, you'll knock my hat off!' protested the Wicked Witch.

Laughing together, the two of them walked down the avenue from the nurses' home and along the dark drive at the back of Maternity, past the deserted pharmacy and the lighted windows of the laboratory and blood bank. They reached the medical residency, ablaze with light and the sound of music. Admiring glances followed them up the stairs to the first-floor corridor and Nicholas Lisle's room, which was crowded to capacity.

'My God!' he exclaimed as they entered, looking

excitingly unfamiliar. 'Fay, darling, you look fabulous—oh, boys, is this going to be a great night!'

And indeed the Hallowe'en party turned out to be a memorable event.

When they went into the common-room, the girls stared in surprise at the spooky cavern it had become. Candles inside hollowed-out pumpkins and lanterns suspended from wall-brackets gave out a flickering light that was reflected in the metallic stars round the walls and a huge, shimmering moon that hung from the ceiling and slowly revolved. In the corner opposite the bar stood a skeleton, its skull grinning with a weirdly phosphorescent glow. A large hi-fi music centre was playing a tape of popular songs, and a crowd of witches and warlocks were either chatting or dancing: the party was under way.

There was no doubt that Batman was the success of the evening, and his acrobatics as he skimmed round the room, jumping up on tables and making a grab at every girl in sight, greatly added to the fun of the party. Charge Nurse Baines of ITU was not called Randy Ron for nothing, and he had set out with the intention of kissing every woman at the party—doctor, nurse, physiotherapist and whoever was female.

'Gotcher, my little beauty!' he growled as he grasped Fay round her tiny waist and lifted her up above his head with a flourish worthy of Nureyev.

'Watch it, Ron, or I'll turn you into a cross-eyed toad!' she threatened from her lofty position above his black-helmeted head and long pointed ears.

'No, turn him into something *different*!' roared the onlookers.

Fay twisted her agile body and sat herself on Ron's shoulders; giving him a sharp dig in the ribs with her foot, she rode him triumphantly round the room amid cheers and applause.

'That's enough, Fay, get down now,' ordered Nicholas as Batman galloped past with a blood-curdling yell, the Wicked Witch perched aloft. She grimaced at Lisle, and defiantly rode round the room a second time, smiling and waving like a circus entertainer—until Ron suddenly sank to his knees, and, leaning forward, sent her flying over his head on to the floor, her long black dress in disarray.

Nicholas was at her side, pulling her to her feet.

'Damned fool! He could have seriously injured you, Fay!' he objected angrily. 'Come along, let's go and get some supper.'

Taking her firmly by the arm, he led her to the buffet table where witches and warlocks were jostling for savouries and salad.

Rose Gillis was the next to be pursued by the indefatigable Ron, though she was speedily rescued by Dr Paul Sykes, one of the registrars from General Surgery who had been admiring the Wicked Queen for some time, and was delighted by this opportunity to grab her by force from her bat-winged assailant.

'That Baines character needs taking down a peg or two,' grumbled Nicholas. 'I don't care for the way he's treated you and Rose. No respect at all—bloody male nurse!'

'I notice that you didn't rush to *my* rescue,' replied Fay coolly.

By one o'clock half the company had drifted away. Hospital parties tended to end earlier than most, with nurses having to get up to be on duty by seven forty-five a.m., and doctors facing long periods of being on call. Even Batman had given up and disappeared.

Fay and Nicholas were dancing to recorded guitar

music, swaying slowly to the rhythm as he held her close, nuzzling his lips against her neck. His fingers lightly stroked the downward curve of her spine, descending to rest on her firm little backside. She felt unrelaxed, her thoughts whirling in confusion and uncertainty. She had refused to drink any more than the two Martinis that had lasted her through the evening, but now her head ached and she longed for the privacy of her room in the nurses' home where she could try to sort out her conflicting emotions.

They stopped dancing, and he sank into an armchair, pulling Fay on to his knee where she perched rather primly as they shared a bowl of potato crisps.

'There's some pasta salad left on the buffet table,' she said. 'I'll go and grab a plate and a couple of forks——'

'No, no, you don't need any more to eat, darling, or you'll get fat,' he murmured, looking up at her with frank anticipation in his lazy blue eyes. 'Mm-mm, I'm sleepy, aren't you?'

'It's all the drink you've downed,' she replied bluntly, scooping up a handful of crisps and trying not to feel repelled by this flushed and pawing man, so different from the enthusiastic exponent of natural childbirth, her possible future employer, partner and who knew what more besides. . . Over at the bar she was surprised to see that Batman had returned, looking amazingly fresh and alert. Ron Baines certainly had stamina!

Nicholas ruffled her hair and kissed the tip of her nose.

'Steady on, I don't care much for this sort of thing in public,' she protested.

'Don't you, angel? Then what about a little of this

sort of thing in private? My room's still where it was before—and empty.'

'No, thank you,' she said hastily, making a move to get up from his lap. Instantly he tightened his hold upon her, and she realised that he had drunk enough to turn quarrelsome if she struggled. Both his arms were clasped round her waist, his fingers firmly interlocked.

This is going to end with a very silly argument, she thought in dismay—and I'm definitely not going to his room. Oh, Rose, where are you? Come and rescue me!

But the Wicked Queen was nowhere to be seen, and Fay felt quite ridiculous, imprisoned in Lisle's arms in full view of the remainder of the party, now draped around the room, mainly in couples.

She tried to unclasp Lisle's hands, but he locked them even more tightly together, pressing hard against her just below her breasts. She looked wildly round the room, imploring with her eyes to be rescued by anybody bold enough to run the gauntlet of Lisle's stubborn temper. She was conscious of her flushed face and untidy hair, a curly strand falling over one eye. Everybody must think I'm drunk, she thought despairingly.

A student male nurse passed them on his way to the buffet, and caught sight of Fay's beseeching look.

'Er—are you all right, love?' he asked, stopping to see if she genuinely needed help.

'No, I want to leave and get away!' she whispered fiercely, adding under her breath to Lisle, 'For heaven's sake let me go, Nicholas!'

'You'd better let her go, mate,' the young man threatened.

'What the hell's it got to do with you, sonny? Stop pestering the lady, will you? She's with me!'

Lisle's voice was loud and belligerent, and faces

turned in their direction. Fay felt utterly undignified, and was ready to cry with vexation. She was at her wit's end when she saw the dark figure at the bar turn round and look directly at them.

And then there seemed to be nobody else in the room but the menacing figure of Batman who stretched his lithe body, and his wide, bat-winged cape spread out on either side as he began to move. Even the smooching couples looked up in awe as the black form swooped towards the armchair where Fay sat helplessly in Lisle's tight embrace.

He towered above them without saying a word, then, springing forward, he brought his fist down on the side of Lisle's head.

'What the devil—ouch! You bastard, Baines, who do you think you are? *Ouch!*'

Lisle's language became unrepeatable as a further punch landed on the other side of his dishevelled head. He raised his hands to fend off another blow, and Fay thankfully jumped to her feet, only to find herself immediately seized round the waist and swept up in one rapid movement by Batman, who then turned and shot from the room, his cloak swirling out behind him and the astonished Fay firmly clasped in his arms as he disappeared through the doorway. It was all over in less than a minute.

After a brief, stunned silence, a cheer went up from the last remaining witches and warlocks.

'Batman strikes again! Hooray!'

'Did you see the way he moved? Talk about a bat out of hell!'

Fay instinctively put her arms around the shoulders of her rescuer, though she was in total confusion at this unforeseen turn of events. One minute she had been trapped in a situation of embarrassment and physical restraint, and in the next she found herself publicly transferred to the equally determined arms of another man—one who was now taking her away by force, and at a quite extraordinary speed. There was a certain sense of exhilaration in being carried in Batman's arms as he ran down the stairs of the residency and along the corridor to the exit, out into the dark, deserted thoroughfare between the main hospital and the out-buildings to the rear.

The night air struck a pleasant chill on her hot face after the stale, smoky atmosphere of the party; it felt deliciously fresh in this first hour of the first day of November. Batman's breath came in short gasps as he dashed swiftly along with Fay's black-gowned body held firmly against him. Even a petite young woman of eight-stone three was a considerable weight for a running man to carry, and this man seemed to have truly superhuman strength. Surely he will have to slow down soon, she thought, he'll need to recover his breath—and then he'll have to release me. I'll thank him for rescuing me, and then run away as quickly as I can to the nurses' home and my room. . .

The thought then occurred to her that she could ask him to put her down now, this very minute, and in fact she could even insist, and start to struggle with him, as she had with Lisle. Yet strangely she felt no wish to protest against this captor: there seemed to be no reason why she should, or why she should want to. She remained wrapped in his arms as he pressed on, her hands clasped behind his helmeted head.

Gradually Fay became aware of an anger in his hold upon her, a seething fury that gave him the strength to go on as his iron fingers dug into her back. She remembered the violence with which he had struck at

Lisle before wrenching her away from him. What could
have made Ron Baines so angry? And where were they
going now? Where was he taking her?

She noticed that he was heading towards the leaf-
strewn avenue that led to the nurses' home, where
Baines had a room in the ground-floor annexe for male
nursing staff. The home seemed the obvious destination for them both—but surely he did not intend to
take her to his room?

And then Fay realised that this man was not Ron
Baines. The knowledge came to her with such absolute
certainty that she wondered why she had not known it
from the moment he had seized her. These shielding
arms which held her with such fierce possession were
not the same arms that had twirled her aloft at the
party. This was a different body, another Batman in
the same black outfit. She could not see the eyes
behind the narrow slits in the helmet, nor was it
possible for her to identify the mouth and nose that
drew rapid, panting breaths through the square cut-
away aperture. It was too dark to see anything clearly
as her head lay against his shoulder: it was a strong,
safe, comfortable shoulder that gave her an unusual
sense of security—and something more. She found
herself wishing that this extraordinary journey need
never end, that they could go on and on through the
darkness with their arms around each other. If only it
could continue in slow motion, as in those wonderfully
effective film sequences. . .there was a timelessness
about this whole experience that was pure magic,
something she had dreamed about but never before
encountered. This man may be in a furious rage, she
thought, but I am enjoying every minute; she tightened
her hold around his neck and shoulders.

Fay's reverie ended with a jolt when he stopped

abruptly halfway along the avenue, within sight of the nurses' home. She slowly unclasped her arms as he lowered her to the ground, though he still encircled her waist with one arm as he leaned back agaist the trunk of a tree. Lightly held against his heaving chest, she could feel his thudding heartbeats as he regained his breath following his tremendous exertion. Again, Fay had the sensation of not wanting to break the spell. Which one of us will be the first to speak? she wondered.

Apart from faintly distant lights still on in one or two windows of the home, they were enveloped in darkness and silence. Neither of them uttered a word, and for the first time the thought came to Fay that her family and friends might consider her to be in a potentially dangerous situation if they could see her now, alone in the middle of the night with a strange man. She would not even be able to identify him if. . .

If what? Rape or some other form of assault? No! She knew intuitively that she had nothing to fear from this man, though she could not have explained exactly how she knew. Completely unafraid, she leaned her dark head against that safe shoulder, and gave a long sigh. They stood there together, neither moving or speaking.

Fay smiled to herself. We must look a very strange pair, she reflected, Batman with his cape and pointed ears, me in my long black dress—a sight to startle any straggling revellers on Hallowe'en! Only there's nobody around, and it's too dark to see anything, anyway. She nestled against his heart. His breathing was becoming slower now, and the rage that had given him such a burst of extra energy was subsiding; she could almost feel it ebbing away in these exquisite shared moments of silent closeness. On a sudden

impulse she put up her hand to touch the masked face.
The body of the suit was of thick acrylic material, but
the helmet, like the gloves, was of soft black leather
and fitted over his head, not attached to the body suit.
Fay wondered if she could lift it off, but decided that
she would have to speak first, reluctant though she was
to break the spell.

'Who are you, Batman?' she asked softly. 'Are you
somebody I know?'

His arm tightened around her, but he did not reply.
She could see the faint glitter of his eyes through the
slits in the helmet.

'Please tell me who you are,' she whispered, smiling
shyly up at him. 'I can't thank a man whose name I
don't know!'

There was another pause before he drew a long
breath and gave a hesitant, muffled answer.

'I'm only somebody who cares about what happens
to you.'

The words were spoken so quietly that Fay could
scarcely hear, but she gave a start of surprise.

Batman was Dr Grant.

No, he couldn't possibly be! Dr Grant was no party-
goer, and besides, he was on call tonight.

But he *was* Lewis Grant.

Yet how could this strong, angry man be dear old
Lewis, so quietly reliable, serious and *safe*? Ah, yes,
she remembered now how she always felt safe with
Lewis around.

'Lewis,' she said very softly, reaching up a hand, 'is
it really you?'

And with a swift movement she slipped her small
hand under the helmet, and lifted it off over his head.
And before she could peer at his face in the darkness,
before she had time to ask another question, her mouth

was covered with his own. Once again her body was gripped by iron hands, and she gave a little cry as her lips were claimed in a kiss of such intensity that she could not resist him, nor deny him a response. She could hardly breathe as he drank from the sweetness of her parted lips. Whipping off the gloves that fell to the ground with the helmet, he gripped her hair, tugging on the unruly curls as he pulled her head back so that he could kiss her chin, her throat, the warm hollow of her neck. Fay was swept along on the tide of his pent-up emotion: it was as if a long-standing dam had given way and let a mighty river come surging through in heaving torrents. Fay could not help but feel her own body respond: involuntarily she raised her hand to touch his face, to grasp the crisp black waves that had been flattened by the helmet—those waves that were greying too soon. Her fingers found his ears, neat and close against his head; she cupped her hands over them, closing her eyes, opening her mouth for him. . .

At last he drew his lips away from hers, and turned his head aside. Still holding her trembling body against his own, he began to murmur brokenly.

'Fay, I'm sorry—I didn't intend this to happen. Really and truly—I didn't. Please forgive me.'

'Lewis—Lewis Grant,' she whispered incredulously. Unable to think of any further words, she added with a weak little smile, 'I thought you were on call tonight.'

'I am. I mean I was, and shall be again soon. Matthew Okoje has taken over my bleep for an hour.'

'Why—why *this*, Lewis?' Fay stammered.

'I came over to the residency to get a book from my room, and I ran into Ron Baines in the men's room, getting out of his Batman suit,' he told her. 'It sounds ridiculous, I know, but all of a sudden I got this idea of borrowing it from him and going into the party incognito. I asked Matthew to take over my bleep—I just fancied having a bit of a lark, I suppose.'

'Oh, Lewis!' Fay could not help giving an unsteady little laugh. 'You certainly succeeded!'

'Well, not really. As soon as I saw you there with that—that *lout*, I just had to get you away from him there and then. You didn't mind, did you, Fay?'

'No, I didn't,' she assured him firmly. 'It was a great relief. Nicholas had had too much to drink, and I'm sure he'll be sorry about that, but I'm most grateful to you, Lewis, of course.'

'But oh, my God, Fay, I didn't plan *this*. I was only going to get you away from a situation that was so completely unworthy of you. Listen, my dear, you're going to have to forget what happened just now. I've no right, no claim on you. Forgive me, Fay, and forget it. It won't happen again.'

Fay listened in mounting astonishment. How could Lewis Grant expect her to forget tonight's scene and their incredible exchange? She would never be able to regard him in the same way as before, not after such uncharacteristic behaviour on his part.

And yet was it so untypical? She thought of the strange encounter they had had in the ward kitchen a couple of weeks previously, when she felt he had come near to kissing her. Maybe she had totally misjudged him. Her thoughts were in confusion: his words and actions seemed to be totally at variance. How *could* she forget that this had happened? And what was there to forgive him for? Kissing was not a crime! And yet— *Lewis Grant*. It was unbelievable.

'It's all right, Lewis,' she heard herself saying shakily. 'It's been such an unexpected night in every way, and I just can't take it all in. I—I just don't know what to say——'

'Don't say anything more,' he cut in. 'I'll take you up to the nurses' home now, and let you get to your room. Come on, Fay, let me see you safely indoors.'

And taking her arm, he led her the rest of the way along the dark avenue, holding his helmet and gloves in his free hand. It was like another transformation: the passionately angry Batman had turned into familiar Dr Grant, the quiet anaesthetist whom everybody liked, and who was treating her with his usual grave courtesy.

They walked up the steps to the front entrance.

'Sleep well, Fay, and don't worry. When we meet again at our work, I shall behave as if this had never happened.'

'So will I, Lewis, if that's what you want. But let me thank you again for getting me away from that party tonight.'

She held out her hand, and he shook it briefly, then quickly raised it to his lips for a moment. There was no lingering in the doorway as Fay pressed the secret combination of numbers that unlocked the door of the home.

'Goodnight, Lewis——' But when she turned to give him a last smile he had disappeared into the dark.

On reaching her room, Fay felt both exhausted and over-excited at the same time. It had been a very long day since she had got up and gone on duty till five p.m.—and then the increasing tensions at the party, culminating with Lisle's boorish behaviour and her amazing abduction by Batman—and even more amazing sequel. She shook her head in disbelief as she quickly undressed and went to take a shower. She cleaned her teeth, put on her nightie and crept into her welcoming bed at nearly two o'clock. Her restless brain was full of jumbled images and contradictory thoughts;

in trying to sort out her feelings towards Nicholas Lisle, she could only remember the comforting arms of the second Batman. Was it possible that Lewis really cared about her in that special way? If his kiss was anything to go by, there seemed to be no doubt about it. And yet he had asked her to forgive him, and seemed anxious that she should try to forget that it had ever happened.

As Fay tossed and turned, her thoughts suddenly changed direction and centred on her friend Susannah Starr. With a gasp of dismay she felt almost certain that Sister Pardoe's suspicions were justified. Oh, poor Susannah! Whatever would she do if Quentin did not return to her? And what could she, Fay, do to help her friend?

With Susannah's face at the centre of her whirling thoughts, sleep suddenly claimed her, and she sank into deep oblivion for many hours.

CHAPTER FOUR

FAY was not due back on duty until one o'clock the following day. She slept through the clamour of bells and alarm clocks that called the nurses from their beds, and the sound of newsreaders and disc jockeys on an assortment of radios. Doors banged and footsteps hurried from the home, leaving comparative silence until the arrival of the night staff coming off duty, when baths were run and Radio Manchester filled the air once again.

Fay heard nothing of these comings and goings as the hands on her bedside clock crept round to a quarter to ten; then a couple of sparrows began a dispute outside her window, and it was their insistent chirping that eventually roused her. She stirred, her eyelids fluttered, and then she sat bolt upright in bed. The memory of last night flooded back, and her first reaction was that it must all have been a dream; her second was relief to find herself alone in her room, refreshed by nearly eight hours of sleep. She got out of bed and drew back the curtains: it was a fine, clear autumnal day.

Fay got dressed, putting on a blue sweater and a pair of corduroys. She made coffee and toasted a slice of bread in the little kitchen down the corridor. She thought of Susannah, who would be on duty now, and decided to take a brisk walk around Beltonshaw Park to clear her head and sort out her confused emotions.

Buttoning a short duffle jacket over her sweater, she ran smartly downstairs and out of the home, along the avenue where last night the incredible scene with Batman had taken place. Her heart beat a little faster as she passed the tree where they had stood together, and she remembered how she had wished that time would stand still, so that the moment could go on and on. . .her footsteps slowed as Lewis Grant's words re-echoed in her head.

He had asked her to forgive him, to behave as if nothing had happened. How could she possibly forget, when every nerve in her body thrilled at the remembrance of those kisses, that fierce embrace from such an unfamiliar Dr Grant? Why had he gone to such trouble to rescue her from an embarrassing situation, and where had that demanding passion come from? If he cared so much about her, why had he been so insistent that the incident should be forgotten and not mentioned again? As Fay continued her walk, she honestly tried to work out an answer to these puzzling questions, and after considering last night's events carefully in the clear light of day she came up with a possible explanation.

From what she knew about Lewis Grant, he tended to set himself apart from the mainstream of hospital life, as if there was some far-reaching happening in his past that made him avoid close relationships. Fay nodded to herself and her dark eyes softened: it had to be a woman, she decided, some woman he had loved very deeply but who had gone out of his life for some reason—married to another man, perhaps, or she might have died. Lewis might even have been married to her, and unable to recover from the grief of widowerhood. Yes, that must be it, thought Fay, a lost love—and maybe she reminded him of his loss because of a physical resemblance. Of course! That would explain why he had kissed her with such aching desire before recollecting himself and apparently regretting it. She must have recalled to mind the happiness of a past love, and that had stirred him to act in such an uncharacteristic way.

A tender little smile curved her lips, and her generous heart hoped that he had enjoyed the few brief moments of re-living his memory, deliberately imagining her to be someone else. She was glad she had been able to reward him in that way for his assistance. It would not be easy to behave as if it had never happened, but, if that was what he wanted, she would do her best to oblige him.

Briskly skirting round the front of the hospital and outpatients' department, Fay suddenly heard her name called. She turned and saw Dr Lisle at the entrance to the antenatal clinic where the morning session was in progress. His face was pale, and he had a bruise above his left eye.

'Fay! Can you spare a moment?'

She thought of the waiting mothers, some with fidgety toddlers running round the clinic, and had no wish to cause them any further delay.

'Good morning,' she said coolly as she approached the doorway.

'Fay, love, about last night. I'm sorry about the way it all ended. It was a total misunderstanding, and I hope you weren't upset.'

'I don't think I misunderstood you at all, Nicholas,' she replied with a direct look. 'And I hope your hangover isn't affecting your concentration this morning.'

'Not at all, I'm fine. Perhaps one less Scotch might have been a good idea, but I was perfectly sober, and there was no need at all for that charge nurse from

ITU to come interfering with us in the way that he did. It was no business of his whatever.'

Fay did not know how to reply, and glanced away.

'However, Fay, I'd like to let you know that I don't intend to make a complaint about Baines, mainly for your sake and not to make an issue of it. I'm prepared to forget it. And Fay——'

'That's good, because you'd look extremely silly if you accused Ron Baines,' she retorted. 'I mustn't keep you from the clinic session—those poor mothers have to wait around quite long enough. Bye!'

She walked away without a backward glance, but her irrepressible sense of humour responded to the funny side of the situation, and she could not resist a quiet chuckle to herself. Poor old Nicholas! No doubt he'd feel that neither his apology nor his generous attitude had been properly appreciated, but Fay could not help that. She knew that in future she would be much less easily impressed by his fine, self-confident views—and she had made up her mind that her future career did *not* include the Lisle Birthing Clinic.

A walk in the park, ankle-deep in fallen leaves, and a browse around the stalls of Beltonshaw Market restored Fay's spirits, but when she returned to duty at one she soon realised that she was at the centre of raging hospital gossip.

Sister Pardoe looked up with an oddly questioning expression as Fay entered the shared office. Staff Nurse Laurie Moffatt, a large, well-built blonde girl, was seated at the antenatal desk, and had obviously been entertaining the older midwife with a lively account of the party. Fay hung up her cloak behind the door, and adjusted her white cap in the wall mirror.

'Aye, ye may well set your cap straight, Sister

Mitchell! I'll be interested to hear your own account of Hallowe'en.'

'Now, don't start on me as soon as I set foot in the door, Sister, dear!' protested Fay in mock reproach. 'Here am I, a model of efficiency and dedication, and in perfect condition, all ready to take over the antenatal ward from Staff Nurse Moffatt. So what's new, Laurie?'

The blonde girl grinned knowingly. 'Sister Pardoe can't wait to hear what happened after you were carried off by Ron Baines! Go on, tell us—what was he like?'

To her annoyance, Fay found herself blushing scarlet.

'Absolutely *nothing* happened, and I'd rather you didn't go spreading silly rumours around,' she answered with a frown.

'Huh! You won't get many people to believe *that*, knowing Mr Baines's reputation!' laughed Laurie with a wink at Sister Pardoe.

'But perhaps you don't know *my* reputation, which is that I don't fool around with the likes of Ron Baines,' returned Fay coldly. 'My interests lie elsewhere.'

As soon as the last four words were uttered, Fay regretted them. They had just slipped out in her embarrassment and indignation at Laurie's suggestion that she had gone off with Ron Baines last night. Whatever must Sister Pardoe think of her?

'O-ho, tell us more!' jeered Laurie. 'And where exactly *do* Sister Mitchell's interests lie, may we ask?'

'No, you may not. Just give me the antenatal ward report, please,' rapped out Fay.

'All right, there's no need to speak to me in that tone, Sister——' began Laurie, but Sister Pardoe cut in sharply.

'Give Sister the report and then go to your lunch, Staff Nurse.'

Laurie shrugged and sulkily obeyed. When she had flounced out of the office, the Scotswoman nodded sagely.

'I think ye'll have quite enough questions to answer about the party, Sister Mitchell, without having to say any more now.'

Fay gave her a grateful glance, and before going off duty the senior midwife briefly outlined the staff situation in the consultant delivery unit that afternoon.

'Sister Starr is on until five. She has one patient in labour, a primigravida,' Fay was told. 'There are two student midwives on duty and a nursing auxiliary, so I don't expect she'll need any help—but maybe you and she will find some time for a little chat this afternoon, over a cup of tea.'

She gave Fay a meaningful look, then put on her cloak and hurried away to the canteen and her half-day off. Left alone in the office, Fay sighed. How silly she had been to allow Laurie Moffatt's light-hearted words to upset her! The girl had only repeated what everybody else must be saying about herself and Ron Baines. She wondered how *he* was reacting today to the wisecracks about the adventures of Batman!

She gave herself a little shake. What you need, my girl, is a good dose of other women's problems, she told herself firmly as she went to do a leisurely round of the antenatal patients, marooned in hospital with unforeseen complications such as toxaemia, low-lying placenta, babies too small for their dates, anaemia, infections and the effects of general social deprivation. Among Fay's patients there were young single girls still at school, deserted wives and those whose husbands were unemployed; Fay knew that one woman's husband was in prison, although she told the others that he was working away from home. Quite a few were heavy smokers, there were occasional heavy drinkers, and drug addiction was not unknown among them. It was women like these, battling daily with poverty and ignorance, who tended to need extra rest and observation in hospital during their pregnancies.

Fay put on a radiant smile as she went into the ward.

'Hi, girls! Great to see you again! Have you been good while I've been away?'

'Ah, it's that nice young sister who always cheers us up!' smiled tired-looking Mrs Pearson to the pretty teenager in the next bed. 'She'll sort you out, Rachel, and talk to your mum, don't worry.'

'How was the party, Sister? Did you and Dr Lisle enjoy yourselves?' asked a voice from the bottom of the ward where a knot of patients were talking together.

'Oh, it was OK,' answered Fay easily.

'I bet it was! Staff Nurse Moffatt has been telling us about Batman!' teased Mrs Pearson with a wink at the others.

Fay joined in the good-humoured laughter. 'Don't believe everything you hear, girls. I'll tell you one thing for sure—I'm really glad to be back here with my ladies-in-waiting!'

And she honestly meant it.

CHAPTER FIVE

FAY sat at the office desk, patiently listening to young Rachel Bamford's mother.

'Of course, Rachel's not the only one, I'm only too well aware of that, Sister,' sighed Mrs Bamford, who wore a quietly expensive suede car coat over her pure wool two-piece suit. Fay was longing for a chance to have a chat with Susannah, but knew that this woman needed to talk. Fay felt particularly sorry for Mrs Bamford who was on the board of governors at Beltonshaw Girls' Grammar School where Rachel was halfway through her A-level course; what a blow it must have been to her and her general practitioner husband when Rachel had broken the news! In many families the unmarried pregnant daughter scarcely raised an eyebrow these days: with or without boy-friends, a steady stream of girls came into Maternity to have their babies which they then proudly took home to show to all their friends; but for a family like the Bamfords it was still a tragedy.

'You've spoken with our Mrs McClennan, I expect?' prompted Fay sympathetically.

'Oh, yes, the social worker—such a charming person, just like yourself, Sister. She's making arrangements for the baby to be taken straight from here to a foster home for six weeks, and then it will go to the adoptive parents. Quite honestly, I don't see why the poor little thing can't go straight to its new parents, but apparently that isn't the policy. With so many couples

60

wanting to adopt, I'm sure that—that the child will make some nice couple very happy.'

Her voice sank to a whisper on the last words, and she bit her lower lip as tears welled up in her eyes.

'I think a cup of tea would be in order, don't you?' suggested Fay, getting up. 'Do you take milk and sugar, Mrs Bamford?'

'Milk, please, no sugar. I'm sorry, Sister, you must see so many of us parents whose girls have. . .all because of some wretched party at some other girl's home. I can't tell you how much we're all longing for it to be over and done with, so that Rachel can get back to her studies and hopefully on to university. The headmistress has been wonderful, and her teachers have sent Rachel plenty of homework to keep her occupied. Of course, it isn't so easy to study in here, now that she's got this problem with her blood-pressure. Still, it won't be for much longer, will it?'

Fay briefly touched Mrs Bamford's shoulder before going into the ward kitchen opposite the office and plugging in the electric kettle. Whatever would we women do without tea? she wondered. She was very sorry for the Bamfords, and sceptical about the adoption plans. There were very good reasons for the six-week fostering period which preceded adoption, and Fay doubted that Rachel's baby would even get that far, because as soon as the girl saw her child and held it she would beg to be allowed to keep it, and her parents would be unable to deny her. Fay sighed. She had seen it all before, so many times—but, for the time being, poor Mrs Bamford must be allowed to cling to her belief that after her grandchild's birth everything could go back to where it was before, with a university degree beckoning to pretty, high-spirited Rachel.

When Fay returned to the office with two cups of tea

on a tray, she hesitated and caught her breath for a moment: Dr Grant was seated at the desk, chatting with Mrs Bamford, who was actually smiling.

Fay composed her face into a professional smile, telling herself that she was pleased to get their first meeting after last night over so soon, and in company.

'I didn't realise that you were on call this afternoon, Dr Grant,' she remarked. 'I'll have to get another cup!'

When she returned with a third cup of tea, he looked up and smiled.

'Thank you very much, Sister Mitchell. This lady has just asked me what an anaesthetist is doing in a maternity department!'

'Ah,' replied Fay, meeting his steady grey eyes and following his train of thought. Neither of them wanted to frighten Mrs Bamford with talk of Caesarean sections, retained placentas or other obstetric emergencies.

'We just never know when we're going to need an anaesthetist in this place, Mrs Bamford, so we keep well in with our gas-men, as we call them! Actually, Dr Grant will probably be needed to give an epidural anaesthetic to one of our patients before today is over. It's becoming a popular form of pain relief, and he gives a very good one!'

'Oh, yes? My husband isn't too keen on the idea of them—of course, there was nothing like that when he did his training, and I only had an injection and gas-and-air when Rachel was born,' said Mrs Bamford doubtfully.

'They weren't in general use until about ten years ago, and they've become much more efficient since then,' explained Fay.

'Yes, I get plenty of practice, that's why I'm so good at them!' laughed Lewis, nodding to Mrs Bamford and putting his finger to the side of his nose in a comically boyish gesture. She visibly relaxed and gave them both a grateful look.

'You've made me feel much happier,' she said with real feeling. 'It's such a comfort to know that Rachel will be in good hands when——' She left the sentence unfinished.

'If you like, I'll have a chat with Rachel about the various kinds of pain relief when the time comes,' offered Lewis as he stirred his tea.

'That would be so good of you, Dr Grant,' replied Mrs Bamford. 'Do you always go to so much trouble for your patients?'

'I always enjoy working on Maternity,' he assured her. 'By the way, Sister, I meant to tell you that I was called into Intensive Therapy this morning, to see a poor old chap who needed a tracheostomy. While I was there, I had a word with the charge nurse—what's the fellow's name? Er—you know who I mean—Baines, that's the one.'

Fay stared very hard at her half-empty cup.

'Very reasonable chap,' went on Lewis casually. 'I had some tackle of his to return, and gave him a tenner for the use of it. I told him not to take any notice of rumours going round, and advised him to answer all queries with a firm, "No comment." He agreed that the less said, the better. And I understand that no further action is going to be taken from another quarter, so that seems to be that. Thought I'd let you know.'

'Thank you.' Fay's voice was barely audible.

'Oh, my goodness, how awful of me to sit here while you two busy people are trying to discuss a confidential case!' exclaimed Mrs Bamford in confusion as she rose hurriedly. 'I'll just go and say goodbye to Rachel, and

then I'll be going. Good afternoon, Sister Mitchell—
Dr Grant—I'm most grateful to you both!'

And she was gone, leaving them alone.

'Poor woman,' commented Fay, and went on
quickly, 'I really appreciate you going to see Ron
Baines, Lewis. The man must be feeling utterly bewildered if he's hearing half the tales that are going round
here!'

They caught each other's eye, and Fay smiled in
spite of her embarrassment.

'You must be feeling terribly tired today,' she
remarked after a short, awkward pause.

'Fay.'

The single word made her draw a sharp breath, and
she was taken aback by his expression, so lively and
animated, his usually grave eyes sparkling, his very
complexion glowing with warm vitality.

'Tired, Fay? I can't remember when I last felt so
damned good!'

She was gazing at him open-mouthed with astonishment when Beryl the nursing auxiliary put her head
round the office door.

'Sister Mitchell, can you come over to CDU, please?
Sister Starr needs you!'

Fay immediately rose and followed her to Stage-One
Room B where Mr Rowan the senior obstetric registrar
was studying the graph of the baby's heartbeat being
recorded by the monitor. On the other side of the
patient's bed stood Susannah. She turned huge,
haunted eyes towards Fay.

'We shall probably be going into Theatre with this
lady,' she said in a low tone. 'Foetal distress. Type two
dips and meconium staining at six centimetres
dilatation.'

'Right-oh,' nodded Fay. 'Shall I prepare her while

you open up the theatre? What's her name?' she added in a whisper.

'Ruth Chalmers. Her husband's out in the waiting-room.'

Having decided on emergency Caesarean section, Mr Rowan contacted the paediatrician and Dr Okoje, who was on call for anaesthetics, to Fay's surprise. She realised that Lewis had made a special visit to Antenatal during his free time just to let her know about his meeting with Ron Baines.

Within ten minutes Ruth Chalmers was being wheeled into the little maternity theatre, and in another five she had been safely delivered of a baby girl by Mr Rowan, assisted by Dr Rose Gillis and Sister Starr, with Dr Okoje as anaesthetist. Fay took the baby from the arms of the paediatrician at the theatre door, and softly called to Mr Chalmers, who was standing white-faced in the theatre annexe.

'Hi, there, Dad! Come and have a look at your little daughter!'

The young man stepped forward apprehensively.

'Is Ruth all right? Oh, my God, what that girl's been through, Sister! And I've really felt for her this afternoon!'

'Sit down, then, and I'll give you the baby to hold,' said Fay. 'Yes, Ruth's fine, but she's fast asleep right now. You're the first to see the baby—it's a privilege that fathers get when there's a Caesarean!'

As he awkwardly took the baby in his arms, and gazed down at the bright little eyes peeping out from the white towel and blanket, the theatre door was flung open and a student midwife called urgently to Fay.

'Please come at once, Sister—Sister Starr has fainted!'

Quickly instructing the new father to hold on to his

baby, Fay kicked off her shoes and tied a face-mask over her nose and mouth. She dashed into the theatre where she took in the situation at a glance.

Susannah was lying full-length on the floor beside the operating table, with Matthew Okoje kneeling beside her, moistening her lips with a piece of damp gauze. Dr Gillis had taken over the duties of the anaesthetist, and Mr Rowan was simply coping on his own with the suturing procedure, helping himself to needles and threading material from the precisely arranged instrument tray.

'Will you take over from Sister Starr, Fay, my dear?' he asked with the calmness and poise of a well-experienced surgeon. 'And get switch to bleep another anaesthetist—Dr Okoje seems rather upset by all this, otherwise everything's under control. Thank God the baby was out already—poor Susannah just managed to stay upright long enough.'

Fay rapidly scrubbed her hands and arms at the wash-basin, then pulled a sterile green gown over her uniform. With slightly trembling hands she drew on a pair of latex gloves, and took Susannah's place at the operating table.

Lewis Grant came in at that moment, and took over from Rose Gillis, who then had to re-scrub and re-gown.

Susannah moaned faintly and managed to sit up, resting her dark head languidly against Matthew's shoulder.

'Right, Sister, I'll help you to stand up now, and we'll get you out of here,' he told her. 'Thanks a lot for taking over, Lewis.'

As he helped the girl to her feet, he whispered to her, and Fay gasped behind her mask as she caught some of the words.

'Courage, my love. . . I've got you safe. . . *I* shan't desert you, no way. . .'

He supported the hollow-eyed girl with his arm, and they left the theatre together, she looking utterly stricken, he with an oddly triumphant expression in his eyes, though there was a grimness too.

Fay's heart sank. How could she not have guessed her friend's predicament? Poor, innocent, trusting, church-going Susannah who had no mother to worry about her, as young Rachel Bamford did: whatever would she do? Fay wondered how she could best help her friend during the difficult months ahead.

When Ruth Chalmers and her baby had been transferred to the post-natal ward on the ground floor, and the theatre cleaned and refurbished, Matthew returned and took Fay aside in the office.

'She's in her room in the nurses' home, but should not be left alone, Sister Mitchell,' he told her anxiously. 'She says she does not want to see anybody, but please go to her, Fay, *please*, as soon as you can. She needs a good woman friend, and if there is anything I can do to help let me know.'

Fay's heart ached as she looked into his sorrowful eyes and saw that he knew.

Rushing over to the nurses' home during her half-hour tea-break at half-past four, she made straight for her friend's room. It was locked.

'Let me in, Susannah. It's Fay.'

'Please go away,' answered a feeble voice, and Fay felt a shiver of fear.

'Let me in *at once*, Susannah, or I shall go and fetch the warden to unlock this door with the master key,' she demanded sharply.

She heard the bed creak, and, to her enormous relief, Susannah opened the door. Fay went in and re-locked it; she sat down on the bed where Susannah lay, hiding her face.

'Fay, you don't understand, there is nothing that anybody can do to help me.' She spoke in a flat, despairing tone.

'Oh, Susannah, I *do* understand, and there's plenty I can do to help you,' insisted Fay, taking hold of her hand. 'You're about three months pregnant, aren't you? And there's no sign of Quentin, right?'

She was hardly prepared for the reaction to this deliberately blunt statement. Susannah almost screamed as she sat up and threw both arms round Fay, and her sobs shook the bed. Yet there was also a wild relief in breaking her silence at last, and tears came to Fay's eyes too as she realised the extent of her friend's despair. For several minutes she rocked the Trinidadian girl in her arms, stroking the tight black curls and cursing her lack of observation over the past weeks.

'Shh, shh, it's not the end of the world, love,' she soothed. 'In this day and age, there's no need to make such a to-do! Think how many single girls we see in here all the time—Rachel Bamford and such a lot more. We'll get through it together, you'll see. When are you due—it must be about May, right?'

'I've worked out May the seventh,' muttered Susannah, mopping her eyes with a handful of tissues.

'And does Quentin know?' asked Fay gently.

'I've written several times, but all I've had from him since he left is two postcards. I don't think he is really interested in me, and—oh, Fay, I love him so much!'

It was just as well that Susannah could not see her friend's grim expression, but Fay kept her voice calm and matter-of-fact.

'Well, now, we'll have to get you organised. I'll come

with you to Mr Horsfield's booking clinic, and we'll see Mrs McClennan at the same time. And I suggest we see Miss Clothier first of all, to let her know.'

'Oh, my God,' moaned Susannah.

'All being well, you should be able to work up to your twenty-eighth week, and then go on fully paid maternity leave,' went on Fay, whose experience with antenatal patients was now all centred upon her friend's needs.

'But where can I *go*, Fay? I can't stay here, in this home, can I?'

'Look, Susannah, I've been thinking for some time that I've lazed around in this place for long enough. What about us two looking out for a nice little flat in Beltonshaw—somewhere where we can have a bit of peace and privacy, and be independent? Good heavens, the more I think about it, the more I wonder why we haven't done it ages ago! Do you know, I'm looking forward to this baby already!'

Susannah raised haggard eyes to look into her friend's face.

'Fay, how can I say thank you? For the first time I feel as if there is a little bit of hope. But oh, how shall I face my friends at church?'

'If they're half as good Christians as you are, love, they'll want to give you all the help they can. Now, wash your face and blow your nose. I'm going to put the kettle on!'

The interview with Miss Clothier the next morning started badly. Fay had rehearsed a pleasing, somewhat flattering speech, and told Susannah to leave the talking to her as they went into the senior midwife's office, but she could not help remembering that the last time she had set foot in this room was to receive a severe reprimand over the birthing-room incident.

'Good morning, Miss Clothier!' she said brightly, with all the polite friendliness she could summon up, while Susannah stood trembling beside her.

'Good morning, Sister Mitchell—Sister Starr,' replied the formidable woman. 'Please sit down. You're fortunate that I've been able to fit you into my very full schedule this morning, and, as you have given me no indication as to why you want to see me so urgently, perhaps you will enlighten me without delay. Sister Starr?'

She turned to Susannah who looked down at the floor and remained silent. Fay began to speak.

'I've come with Sister Starr, Miss Clothier, because——'

The senior midwife held up an imperious hand.

'I was not addressing you,' she said icily.

Fay flushed angrily and glanced at Susannah, who lowered her head and covered her face with her hands. Fay immediately rose and put a protective arm around her friend's shoulders.

'I'm afraid you'll have to address me, Miss Clothier,' she snapped, mentally discarding the speech she had rehearsed. 'I'm here because my friend and colleague Sister Starr is going to have a baby some time around the beginning of May. She is deeply distressed, as you can see, which is why I have accompanied her to tell you.'

Miss Clothier gave a gasp of surprise, and quickly decided to be more approachable.

'Oh, I *see*,' she said in a half-apologetic tone. 'Oh, dear. If only you had given me some idea beforehand, I would have been better prepared. I'll ask my secretary to send in a tray of tea.' She pressed a buzzer on her desk.

And from then onwards the atmosphere improved: over the cups and saucers Miss Clothier was anxious to show herself in a compassionate light, and approved of their plans to move out of the nurses' home.

'Is there any possibility of—er—marriage?' she enquired, and Fay shook her head, although she knew that Susannah still clung to a faint hope that Quentin would reappear in her life.

'I see. Most unfortunate,' sighed Miss Clothier, shaking her permed and tinted head. 'Sister Starr is the very last member of my staff that I would have—yes, I'm very sorry. I'll give you all the help I can, of course, Sister, and I'll be willing to re-appoint you, perhaps on a part-time basis, after your maternity leave. I'll see you alone some time next week, when you've had an opportunity to compose yourself.'

She turned over the pages of her desk diary, and an appointment was duly made. Susannah had hardly spoken a word.

'Right, I think that's all we need to say for the present,' said the senior midwife, rising. 'Try not to be too down-hearted, Sister Starr,' she added with determined brightness. 'It's surprising how these things have a way of working out, you know!'

'Good morning, Miss Clothier,' replied Fay, trying not to grind her teeth. After all, it could have been a lot worse. . .

They returned to the maternity department, where Fay confided in a sympathetic Sister Pardoe.

'Och, never mind about Ann Clothier, she'll be wanting everybody to say how good she is to poor Sister Starr. I'm only glad that something's being done about the lassie. Is she going to Mr Horsfield's booking clinic this afternoon?'

'Yes, and I'll have to go with her,' answered Fay. 'She's got a half-day, but I'm down to work this afternoon. Could you possibly change with me, Sister Pardoe?'

'No problem. You go off at twelve-thirty, Sister, and come back at five. I'll work through this afternoon.'

'Thanks, Sister Pardoe, you're a brick,' said Fay gratefully. 'Poor Susannah! It's going to be another ordeal for her.'

'Aye, but it's got to be faced,' replied the Scotswoman. 'It'll be a nine-day wonder, and then there'll be something else to talk about, you'll see! At least it will eclipse the adventures of Batman!' she added with a sly little smile.

Before Fay could reply, a white-coated figure appeared at the office door.

'Morning, Sister Pardoe. If you could spare Sister Mitchell for a few minutes, I'd be glad of a quick word with her.'

'Of course, Dr Grant. Excuse me, I have to check the stores,' replied the tactful senior sister, quietly leaving the office and closing the door behind her.

'Bless her, she must have known that what I've come to say isn't going to be easy,' murmured Lewis, and Fay sensed the tension in his voice and manner.

'Can I offer you a cup of coffee?' she ventured.

'No, thanks, Fay, I'm due in Main Theatre soon. Look, it's about Susannah. Matthew and I have been talking about her.'

'Oh.' The single syllable hung in the air while she waited for his next words.

'Oh, Fay, Matthew's in one hell of a state over all this, and he wants me to tell you that if there's anything—*anything* he can do to make life a little easier for her, you've only to let him know. To put it bluntly, he's not short of money, and so if there's any problem when she has to take time off—I mean with rent and heating, for example——'

Fay's eyes were suddenly misty, and she averted her face. After the confrontation with Miss Clothier, the Ugandan doctor's genuine loving concern was heartwarming, not only because of his practical generosity, but for his delicacy: it must have cost him an effort to ask Lewis to act as go-between.

'Fay, my dear, are you all right?'

She turned shining eyes to him. 'How good of Matthew! And you too, Lewis—it can't have been easy to say.'

He regarded her from the other side of the desk with a questioning look.

'We know we can count on you to manage things discreetly, Fay. Matthew cares for the girl so much more than she knows.'

'Even though she's pregnant and has been ditched by the other man?' asked Fay bluntly.

'Of course. Matthew's not the sort to change just because of circumstances. On the contrary, he——' Lewis broke off, biting his lip. 'Fay, do you think that there's any chance of her boyfriend coming back and taking responsibility for her and the baby?'

Fay shook her head slowly. 'I doubt it. He sounds a superficial character, and deceived Susannah completely. She believed everything he told her, but her trust has been betrayed. It happens all the time, but Susannah's such a good, honest girl, and feels her situation much more keenly than most of the unmarried mums we get in here.' She drew a long sigh that ended on a sob. 'Oh, Lewis, it's too bad! This shouldn't have happened to *her*!'

Her voice rose, and her dark eyes blazed. He took a step towards her, but then checked himself with an effort.

'Fay, my dear, please try not to be bitter over what's happened. Susannah might have been deceived and deserted, but, my God, she's still got the love of a good man!'

'No, Lewis, don't say that,' she protested, though deeply moved by his words. 'Right now Susannah feels that the bottom has fallen out of her world, and it's not for us to plan the future for her. She's not in love with Matthew, and would be horrified if she thought that he——'

'Of course, Fay, I'm sorry. I didn't mean to do anything more than pass on his offer of help. He has every respect for her feelings right now.'

She made a sympathetic little gesture with her hands.

'It's all right, Lewis, don't worry. I'm sorry I was so dramatic! Tell Matthew I'll take good care of her, and might even put in a word for him when the stars are favourable!'

'You're an amazing girl, Fay. Whatever would we do without you?' smiled Lewis, and she felt warmed by the tenderness in his voice and expression. What was it about this man that made her feel so safe? He had come to her with a message of love from another man to another woman, yet as she now looked up into his face the unspoken words she saw there were for herself alone. She closed her eyes momentarily, but remembered where she was and assumed a businesslike air.

'I know what! You and Matthew can help us to shift our belongings when we move out of the nurses' home!'

she told him brightly. 'We're going to look for a nice, cosy little flat that we can share.'

'Oh, right! No problem,' he said at once, catching her change of mood. 'I'll start looking for some suitable places in Beltonshaw for you.'

'That's kind of you, but now we mustn't keep poor Sister Pardoe out of her office any longer,' she declared, her face breaking into the impish grin that had pierced his defences when he first met her. As he made for the door, she leaned towards him and whispered teasingly, 'Off you go, Batman—shoo!'

As he hurried down the corridor, nodding to Sister Pardoe who smiled in return, his thoughts raged inwardly, contradicting each other and pulling in completely opposite directions.

Dear, sweet, delicious little Fay! Every instinct within him longed to enfold her close to his heart and never let her go. . .

And another voice told him that he must not. How difficult it was, always to be on his guard, never to let his resolution weaken. Could he be that strong?

Yes, he told himself grimly, he could. Because he loved her too much to share his burden with her.

Susannah was the first patient to be seen in Mr Horsfield's booking clinic that afternoon. Welcoming them both with a handshake, the consultant politely nodded to the antenatal clinic sister, who discreetly withdrew, leaving Fay to act as chaperon during the detailed questioning and the intimate examination. Mr Horsfield's kindly ease of manner was balanced by the cool, matter-of-fact professionalism with which he approached the delicate situation. He asked Susannah if she intended to get married, and when she sorrowfully shook her head he smiled and remarked how much better it was to remain single than to rush into an unwise marriage. Privately he concluded that Matthew Okoje could not be the father, or they would be married by now.

'We must take good care of one of our best mid-wives, my dear,' he told the downcast girl at the end of the examination. 'Have a word with Mrs McClennan, and she'll see that you fill up all the right forms. And you've got the best friend any girl could wish for,' he added, smiling in Fay's direction. 'I rely on you, Sister Mitchell, to look after her and keep me informed—all right?'

Fay nodded in complete understanding: Mr Horsfield was not happy about Susannah's depression.

From the booking clinic they went to the laboratory where blood samples were taken for a variety of tests, and after that came the interview with Mrs McClennan the social worker, who was discreetly sympathetic and helpful.

'I can't remember when I last heard so many ques-tions asked!' exclaimed Fay when at last all the routine procedures were completed, and the two of them headed for the nurses' home. 'Let's go and have some tea, and you must put your feet up, love.'

Susannah smiled resignedly. 'Thanks to you, Fay, I've come a long way since yesterday.'

'That's my girl!' approved Fay, ignoring the start of a headache. 'And tomorrow we'll start flat-hunting—oh, good afternoon, Dr Okoje!' she added quickly as they almost collided with the anaesthetist as he strode out of Accident and Emergency.

'Oh, Sister Mitchell—Sister Starr!' he replied in some confusion, knowing that they had been to the booking clinic, and that the news of Susannah's preg-nancy would rapidly become common knowledge. He realised too that his own name might be whispered in the speculation as to the father's identity.

'Dr Grant spoke to you this morning, I believe?' he said in a low tone to Fay, and she saw the strain in his eyes.

'Yes, Dr Okoje, and I understand,' she murmured.

He glanced at Susannah who had walked a little way ahead, and gave Fay a grateful look before hurrying on. She was touched to the heart, and although she had no intention of applying to him for money she knew that his offer had to be acknowledged. This man truly loved Susannah, even though she did not return his love and was carrying another man's child. Fay secretly wished him well, and hoped that one day he would be rewarded, but for the present she knew that Susannah's wounded heart needed time to recover from the bitterness of Quentin's betrayal.

When Fay returned to the antenatal ward at five, she found Nicholas Lisle in the office; he greeted her excitedly.

'Fay, darling, I've found the very place for the Lisle Birthing Clinic! A splendid four-storey house in Elm Grove, just three miles from the city centre. It'll be the best investment my father will ever make!'

Fay drew back from his exuberant hug as he continued to enthuse about the premises.

'By this time next year it will be well and truly on the map—and there'll be a very special place in it for you, Fay, my little witch,' he added significantly.

'And Miss Clothier?' Fay could not resist asking.

'Ah, now that could be a little bit awkward,' he replied with less enthusiasm. 'Ann's tremendously competent, of course, but perhaps not quite so strong on relationships. I intend to have complete harmony among my staff, and I think Ann's place is here as senior midwife, a useful counter-balance to Horsfield's meddlesome, over-cautious obstetrics.'

Fay remembered Sister Pardoe's prediction that Miss Clothier would be dropped in favour of a younger and more attractive woman to head the Lisle midwifery team. Well, it won't be *me*, she thought.

'There's a lot of work to be done on the place, of course,' he went on. 'Converting, decorating, installing the circular pool for water-births—you'll have to come and look over it with me, Fay. It will be the place of choice in the north for actresses and TV personalities, and we might even attract some of the younger royals once we get established! I can see you now in the colour supplements—"Sister Fay of the Lisle Birthing Clinic"—— *Fay*! Aren't you listening?'

He followed her along the corridor and into the treatment-room where she picked up the oblong metal box containing the instrument used for taking blood-pressures. She put a stethoscope round her neck.

'Excuse me, Dr Lisle. I'm already late with the four-hourly recordings.'

He stared in disbelief that she could be so unmoved by the glittering future he pictured for her.

'What's the problem, Fay? Oh, I suppose you've been knocked off course by this bombshell from your churchy West Indian friend. Clever of her to catch Okoje that way! When's the wedding?'

She wondered how she could ever have imagined herself attracted to this man.

'I have no intention of discussing Sister Starr's business with you. And now if you will just let me get on with my work, please——'

'Hey, not so fast!' he protested, barring her way. 'When are you having dinner with me?'

Fay stood facing him squarely. 'Dr Lisle, I'm going

to be very busy for the next few months, and there won't be time for wining and dining. Now *please* let me pass!'

Her dark eyes flashed, and he rose to the challenge. As she made a dash for the door, he caught hold of her and wrenched the metal box from her hands. There was an undignified struggle as she tried to free herself.

'Come here, you little witch, I know what you need!' he muttered, and to her furious indignation he kissed her lips forcibly and gave her a sharp smack on the backside; he then had to suppress a howl of pain as she kicked his leg as hard as she could. He let her go, and although she was shaking with rage she did not call out or raise her voice. Her first thought was for her antenatal patients only a few yards away at the end of the corridor. However appalling she found such harassment while on duty, she had no wish to cause a scene.

'Let me out of here *at once*, damn you!' she hissed breathlessly as they faced each other. At the sound of approaching footsteps he moved away from the door, and a moment later Lewis Grant looked in. He raised his eyebrows at the sight of Fay's flushed face and untidy hair upon which her cap sat wildly askew. She burned with vexation at what he must think of this compromising scene.

'Well, well, Grant, you seem to be always lurking in this neck of the woods nowadays,' drawled Lisle, as calmly as if he had been merely engaged in idle chat with Fay.

Lewis completely ignored him. 'I'm sorry to interrupt you, Sister Mitchell, but I just called to leave a couple of addresses you might be interested in following up,' he said crisply. 'I'll leave them on the office desk, OK?' He abruptly turned and strode away.

'Thanks a lot, Dr Grant!' Fay called out after him, almost inclined to pursue him and try to explain that appearances were deceptive; but she checked herself, feeling that this would only pile on further humiliation. She picked up the metal box and swept out of the treatment-room to take the four-hourly blood-pressures, her face instantly composed and cheerful for her patients who had no idea of the turmoil that raged behind her smile.

Nicholas Lisle left the department with a thoughtful frown on his handsome face. The little witch was certainly unpredictable! He would have to handle her with more care, he decided; he did not believe that any woman could resist his charm indefinitely. Besides, he liked a challenge: he was so used to easy victories.

CHAPTER SIX

WHEN Fay and the nursing auxiliary had given out the
suppers in the antenatal ward, she did the evening
medicine round and then sat down in the office with a
cup of tea, hoping to take a quick look at the two
addresses that Lewis had left for her. One was in
nearby Conway Road, a comfortable and spacious flat
once occupied by Mr Rowan before he married; the
other was in a new complex of luxury flats that had
been built overlooking Beltonshaw Park.

Fay sipped her tea and frowned. Both of these flats
were completely out of the financial reach of Susannah
and herself, and she suspected that Matthew Okoje
must have offered to make a substantial contribution
to the rent. And that was out of the question, decided
Fay; Susannah would never agree to such assistance,
and she herself did not wish to be under such an
obligation to an unrelated man, however kind. And yet
could it be right for Susannah—and later the baby,
too—to live in much less comfortable accommodation
when there was such a ready, willing offer of something
better?

Fay's head ached, and she felt her courage waver a
little. How long would it take them to find the right
place at the right price? She began to foresee difficulties
ahead, and wondered if she would be strong enough to
cope with all the responsibility she had taken on, in
addition to a demanding full-time job.

Before visiting time, Mrs Pearson was due for half
an hour's foetal heart monitoring. She was in hospital

because the baby was not gaining weight, and tests had shown placental insufficiency. Mr Horsfield had ordered twice-daily monitoring, and although Mrs Pearson had three weeks to go before her expected delivery date Fay felt certain that the consultant would get her delivered earlier, in spite of the baby's small size.

As Fay clicked together the broad elastic straps that held the two sensors in place on Mrs Pearson's tummy, the girl in the next bed began to moan and writhe from side to side. Poor Jody Pockett was an overweight but not over-bright blonde of eighteen who was not due to have her baby until early in the New Year, but had been in and out of Beltonshaw General since halfway through her pregnancy, convinced that the baby was on its way. She had become something of a joke with the ambulance team, but Fay pitied her, knowing how the friendless girl craved attention.

'Poor Jody, you *are* having an uncomfortable pregnancy, aren't you, love?' she said sympathetically. 'But it isn't *proper* contractions that you're getting, it's just your womb tightening up every so often. We call them Braxton-Hicks' contractions, and they're a sort of practice for the real thing. Honestly, Jody, you're not ready to have your baby for another six or seven weeks.'

'Then 'ow come my Mum says I'm bigger than she was when she 'ad me?' muttered Jody sulkily.

'I really couldn't say, dear, only your scan shows a normal pregnancy at just thirty-three weeks. Cheer up, have a shower and a shampoo—it'll make you feel better!'

Jody began to cry. 'Nobody takes any notice of these 'orrible pains I keep getting!' she sobbed. Fay sighed and sat down on the bed.

'Look, love, I'll fetch you a cup of tea and a couple of pain-killing tablets,' she said patiently. 'And if the pains haven't gone by visiting time I'll put you on the monitor, OK?'

'It's two sugars for me in tea,' Jody reminded her, heaving herself over in bed to rummage in her locker for sweets and biscuits. Fay wondered how on earth the girl was going to cope with the baby when it eventually got born.

Returning to the office, she found Lewis Grant at the CDU desk, writing up the details of an epidural; he looked up briefly but did not speak as Fay commenced to write the day report in each patient's nursing records. They were both aware of a certain tension in the air, and could only guess at each other's thoughts.

Just before the visiting time, Fay went to take the monitor off Mrs Pearson, and found to her concern that the foetal heart was below average rate, with intermittent dips on the tracing. She smiled reassuringly at the patient and said she would leave the monitor on for another half-hour, and as soon as she returned to the office she asked the switchboard to bleep Dr Gillis, the obstetric house officer on call. Lewis had finished his writing-up, and was idly glancing at a copy of the *Midwives' Chronicle*.

'Hi, Fay, what a day!' exclaimed Rose Gillis as she came into the office and sat down. 'I haven't stopped for a bite to eat since I grabbed a sandwich and an apple at midday. What's up?'

'Mrs Pearson's tracing is a bit flat, and I don't like it,' replied Fay. 'I'll do you a slice of toast in the kitchen while you go and look at it.'

'Oh, my God, I suppose I'd better ask Nicholas to come and see it,' sighed Rose, getting up and going into the ward. When she returned with the tracing, she bleeped Dr Lisle and gratefully tucked into tea and toast while she waited for him.

'How's Batman?' she asked Fay with a sidelong look.

Fay blushed crimson and did not dare to look in Lewis's direction; he appeared to be deeply engrossed in an article on breast-feeding.

'Busy with his work, I presume, like Superman,' she replied promptly, referring to Dr Sykes the surgical registrar who had spirited away the Wicked Queen of Narnia at the Hallowe'en party. Rose chuckled.

'Well, at least we know Superman's name,' she rejoined, 'whereas Batman could be one of several I've heard suggested. Come on, Fay, open your heart to an understanding woman doctor! It wasn't Ron Baines, was it?'

Fay was rescued by the arrival of Lisle who strode in with a superior air.

'What's all this nonsense about a tracing?' he demanded, picking up the graph paper from the desk and holding it up.

'*That's* all right! The baby's just having a quiet spell. If I had my way, I'd scrap these damned machines for all except a few high-risk mothers in labour!'

Rose Gillis raised her eyebrows, and Fay suspected that part of his bluster was due to embarrassment over their earlier encounter that evening.

'I'll go and have a word with Mrs Pearson,' he said. 'The poor woman must be worried sick by all this fuss. To say nothing of wasting my time!' He left without further comment, and Rose shrugged.

'Oh, well, that's that,' she said. 'I'll go over to Gynaecology and look at today's post-ops. By the way, I'm terribly sorry about Susannah,' she added in a lower tone. 'The very last girl I would have—er——'

'Quite,' said Fay quickly. 'Actually, Rose, I'm going

to leave Mrs Pearson on the monitor a bit longer. I'm not too happy about her, in spite of what Dr Lisle thinks. Call it bad vibes or what you like.'

For a moment her eyes met Lewis's, and she caught his nod of approval.

'Just as you like, Fay, only if you're *still* not happy with the tracing, don't call me, call Lisle!' warned Rose with a wry grimace. She respected Fay's intuition, but found working with Dr Lisle difficult.

Left alone, Fay and Lewis relapsed into silence again, though she found it hard to concentrate on the day report, and her headache persisted. The visitors arrived and a hum of conversation could be heard in the ward. Suddenly the bulky frame of Mr Pearson appeared in the doorway, and they both looked up questioningly.

'Excuse me, Doctor—er—Nurse, but t'wife says yon machine's not working,' he reported. 'Baby's heartbeat's gone reet slow, and she sent me to let you know.'

Fay sprang up and rushed into the ward where Mrs Pearson lay anxiously looking at the tracing. One glance was enough to send Fay flying back to the office and the telephone.

'Get me Dr Lisle,' she told switchboard urgently.

'What will you do if he argues with you, Fay?' asked Lewis.

'If he doesn't come straight away, I'll use the magic word that makes a registrar do as he's told,' she replied grimly.

'Magic word? What might that be?' asked Lewis, amused.

'You'll hear. Remember I'm a witch! Oh, hello, Dr Lisle. Will you come up to Antenatal at once, please?

Mrs Pearson's foetal heart has deteriorated badly, and she probably needs an emergency Caesarean section.'

There was an annoyed gasp at the other end of the line.

'You keep to your job, Fay, and I'll do mine. We've already been through this charade. I'll come up when I've finished my supper——'

Fay saw Lewis's eyes, grey and piercing, fixed intently upon her as she interrupted Lisle's protest.

'Listen to me, Nicholas,' she said quietly, deliberately using his Christian name for emphasis. 'If you don't come up here *immediately*, I will telephone Mr Horsfield at his home. Is that quite clear?'

'*No*! Yes, all right, Fay, there's no need for drama. I'll be right up. Alert the CDU staff, will you? And get hold of Rose to take blood for cross-matching and to put up a drip. Thanks!'

Fay gave Lewis a meaningful glance as she replaced the phone.

'Good girl,' he said admiringly. 'So the magic word is *Horsfield*?'

'Yes, a very quick and effective spell, gets them up here at the speed of light,' she replied, her mouth set in a straight line. Her head throbbed as her anxiety for the Pearson baby increased.

'Come on, Fay, let's get Mrs Pearson out of the ward,' he said, getting up. 'You recall Rose and tell Special Care Baby Unit to stand by for a tiddler. At least *I'm* here already and I'll have a word with the Pearsons about the anaesthetic. All right, love?'

Fay nodded gratefully, thankful for his quiet efficiency without panic. She knew that, with Lewis around, everything would be all right; he always made her feel safe.

The Caesarean section was performed by Dr Lisle,

assisted by Dr Gillis and with Dr Grant as anaesthetist. Mrs Pearson's son was born just as the night staff came on duty, a skinny little fellow whose three-hourly guzzles at the bottle raised his body weight by half a pound in his first two days of life.

As soon as the operation was over, Lisle strode out of the theatre to speak to Fay. He was anxious to exonerate himself with her, but did not want to admit misjudgement.

'Look, Fay, about what you said on the phone—I'm sorry if I sounded a bit offhand, but there was no need for you to panic, you know.'

'I beg your pardon?' she replied coldly. 'I wasn't aware that I panicked. I just took what steps I could to deal with a grave emergency, and it's just as well that I did.'

'Oh, for God's sake, Fay, after I've had one hell of a day!' he protested.

'I doubt if you've had a more trying day than I have,' she muttered, and, wrapping her scarlet-lined cloak around her, she turned away and headed for the stairs.

Lisle called out after her, 'Hey, just a minute, Fay! Wait! Don't take it the wrong way——'

But she was hurrying down the stairs and out into the cool darkness, her eyes full of tears. She felt completely exhausted, and quite unable to face an argument in which she might break down. She heard rapid footsteps behind her, and increased her pace; so did her pursuer.

Utterly exasperated, she turned round to face him.

'For heaven's sake, leave me alone, can't you? Getting a live baby was all I cared about, right?'

She gasped and stared in sudden astonishment.

'*Lewis*! Oh, Lewis, it's you—what must you think of me? Oh, Lewis, Lewis. . .'

For he had almost run into her, and now swept her straight into his arms. Holding her head against his chest, he pulled up the hood of her cloak against the wind.

'All right, all right, everything's fine now, don't worry.' His voice was deeply soothing, and his embrace was that of a friend.

'I'm sorry, Lewis, but it's been such a day—such a long day,' she whispered, her voice hoarse with fatigue.

'I know, I know. And I agree with what you said about getting a live baby. And we did, my love, we did.' He patted her shoulder gently as he spoke.

'I was so worried about the Pearson baby, you see, Lewis.'

'Yes, and Lisle should be grateful,' he replied. 'He owes you thanks and an apology.'

'Oh, I don't want an apology!' She laughed a little shakily.

'Maybe not, but don't let yourself be put at a disadvantage, Fay. Not in any sense of the word.' He briefly tightened his hold on her arm, and she remembered the unpleasant scene with Lisle in the treatment-room earlier; she wondered if Lewis had that in mind. She felt the blood rush to her face, and was thankful for the darkness.

'Now, Fay, you are to go straight to your room in the nurses' home, and to sleep. No chatting tonight, not even with Susannah, do you hear?'

'Yes, Lewis.' She smiled shyly up at him, and he secretly prayed for self-control.

'Do you want me to walk up with you?' he offered, almost hoping that she would refuse.

'Yes, please, if you wouldn't mind,' she said as they linked arms.

Walking up the avenue together in the dark, they

both remembered the last occasion, although neither mentioned it. Was it only the day before yesterday. . .? thought Fay in amazement.

He stopped at the front entrance of the home.

'Goodnight, then, Fay. Remember what I said— straight to bed and to sleep!'

'Yes, Dr Grant!' The little imp of mischief had returned to her eyes.

'Promise?'

'I promise.'

And, standing on tiptoe, she solemnly planted a kiss on his cheek, like a little girl who had no idea of the effect she had on his heart.

The November days passed quickly, and the last ragged brown leaves fluttered down from the trees around the nurses' home and along the avenue. Every hour of each day was filled for Fay, who spent her free afternoons and evenings visiting possible flats. Every place within their price range seemed to have some serious disadvantage: in one the rooms were too big, with rattling windows that let in draughts; in another the shared kitchen facilities were less than hygienic; another house had a disagreeable smell of stale tobacco, and in two others it was made clear that Susannah would not be welcome.

Fay became deeply discouraged, and had almost decided to take one of the better, more expensive flats, accepting Matthew Okoje's offer of help without telling Susannah. As she sat disconsolately on her bed one Sunday evening, a knock on the door interrupted her train of thought, and in sailed Susannah, looking happier and more alive than she had been for many weeks.

'Isn't the world a beautiful place, Fay, with so many good people in it?' she cried with shining eyes.

Fay immediately demanded to know the reason for this transformation, wondering if Quentin had reappeared.

'It's my church, Fay—my wonderful pastor and all the friends who have missed me since I stopped going. You see, I plucked up courage to go to the service this evening, and afterwards there was a meeting in the hall. They asked me what was the matter, and when I told them—oh, Fay——!'

Her voice broke and tears rolled down her cheeks, though her smile persisted like the sun behind rain-clouds.

'They were so kind—so loving, all of them. I've had so many offers this evening, Fay—a pram, a cot, baby clothes and—and money. Apart from you, Fay, dear, I've never known such warmth and generosity—they really *want* to help me, Fay!'

'Oh, how marvellous! I *told* you that they'd rally round you, didn't I, you silly old thing!' exclaimed Fay affectionately as she hugged her friend. 'Thank God, you look like your old self again!'

'No, I shall never be the same as I was, because I've learned so much more than I knew before,' answered the Trinidadian girl with a deep, brooding expression in her eyes. 'This has changed me forever. And for the first time I now feel that I love my baby.'

Fay bit her lip and squeezed her friend's hand; she thought of Matthew, and privately hoped that Quentin would never return.

'But that isn't all—there's more to tell you,' went on Susannah. 'There is a widow who belongs to the church, Abigail Leroy, very quiet and sad, I hardly noticed her before—she just opened her arms to me and held me, Fay, and she says that we can go to live with her! Her house is quite big, and she's all on her own, and lonely.'

Fay opened her eyes wide at hearing this.

'Really? Are you sure that she included me, or is she just offering *you* a home with her?' she asked in some confusion.

'Oh, you and me both, Fay! I told her how good you've been to me. Also I told her what we'd agreed on as a maximum rent, and she says it's more than enough. We can go and look at the house any time, it's not far. Thirty-seven Grange Road.'

'What are we waiting for? She'll be there now, won't she?' cried Fay eagerly, jumping up from the bed and pulling on her duffle jacket.

It needed only one visit to number thirty-seven Grange Road: both house and landlady were agreed to be ideal. Mrs Leroy, a motherly woman of mixed English and Caribbean stock, was as excited as the two young midwives, and offered them the whole of the upstairs floor of the house where she had lived with her husband and brought up her family.

'You can turn the large bedroom into a living-room,' she pointed out.

'Yes, Susannah can have the middle bedroom, and I'll take the small one,' decided Fay.

'No, I have a better idea,' suggested Abigail with a smile. 'There is a little room up in the attic, with a gabled window. You could have that, Fay, and I'll get the small bedroom converted into a nice little kitchen, so that you can prepare snacks—and baby foods, perhaps, when Susannah. . .' She hesitated. 'I mean that Fay wouldn't have to be disturbed.'

The girls were overjoyed, and Fay knew that she would appreciate climbing up into her attic hideaway, while Susannah's sunny, south-facing room would be ideal when the baby arrived.

'I can hardly wait to have a baby in the house again!' confided Abigail, showing them the brightly coloured crocheted squares she was making, to join together into cot-blankets and pram-covers.

In the first week of December the move took place. The girls both had the same day off, and Matthew Okoje arrived early in his small saloon car to transfer their belongings from the nurses' home. He had made two journeys when Nicholas Lisle turned up in his roomy estate car and packed into it the remainder of the clothes, books, pictures, utensils and house-plants that the girls had accumulated. Fay had to accept his assistance with a good grace, as there was no valid reason for declining it; unfortunately Lewis Grant was on call and not able to leave the hospital all day. Fay made an effort to hide her disappointment.

When everything was at last installed at the new address, the two midwives and two doctors sat down to a fish and chip repast, and Nicholas produced a bottle of wine. Fay rose to the occasion as hostess.

'Here's to happy times in our new home,' she said, clinking her glass against each of the other's. 'Cheers, everybody, and thanks to Matthew and Nicholas, our removal men!'

'Here's happiness to Susannah and Fay,' murmured Matthew, stealing a glance at the woman he loved.

'Here's to Sister Fay of the Lisle Birthing Clinic,' said Nicholas with a nod in her direction.

Susannah raised her glass of orange juice and spoke quietly and clearly. 'Thank you, everybody. May you all be rewarded as you deserve. And God bless the lady who has taken us into her home,' she added with a special smile in the direction of the widow who stood beaming upon them from the door. Fay felt that a good move had been made, and was only sorry that Lewis had been unable to share this moment.

Within a week Abigail told the pastor of her church that her lonely life was completely changed. Instead of dreading Christmas this year, she was looking forward to it, she told him. Susannah responded to Abigail's devotion—the tasty West Indian dishes set before her, the fussing with slippers and hot-water bottles when the girl came home from work tired and cold. Fay also relaxed, and realised how grateful she was to Abigail for taking on so much of the responsibility for Susannah's physical and mental well-being.

'Living out suits you, Fay,' remarked Lewis over coffee in the office with Sister Pardoe. 'You were looking very tired and strained, but now you're blooming again, I'm glad to see. Matthew says that the flat is very nice.'

'It certainly is,' agreed Fay. 'Why don't you come and have tea with us one day? Bring Matthew with you,' she added.

He smiled and thanked her, but avoided making a definite commitment to call.

'By the way, the Christmas duty roster is up,' said Sister Pardoe. 'You're working on Christmas Day, Sister, but you've got New Year's Eve and New Year's Day free.'

'Oh, have I?' asked Fay. 'What about *your* Christmas duties, Lewis?'

'Opposite to you, Fay. I'm off from midday on Christmas Eve till midday on Boxing Day, so I'll be going home this year.' There was a tender smile on his lips, and his grey eyes softened. 'But I'm on call all over the New Year,' he added.

'So we won't be seeing much of each other during

the festive season,' said Fay with a small sigh, curious
to know about his Christmas at home, but not feeling
able to ask him.

'Where will you spend the New Year, Sister?' asked
the Scotswoman.

'I might go to visit my father and stepmother up in
Westmorland,' replied Fay thoughtfully.

'I thought you were a Beltonshaw girl,' remarked
Sister Pardoe.

'Oh, I am, and I've never lived anywhere else,' Fay
told her. 'I kept house for my dad and brother after my
mother died. But when Dad re-married he decided to
move further north. Roy—that's my brother—went
into the merchant navy, and that's when I moved into
the nurses' home. I still think of Beltonshaw as home,
even though the house I grew up in belongs to other
people now.'

'Och, you poor wee lass,' sympathised Sister Pardoe.
'And do you get on all right with your stepmother,
then?'

'Oh, yes, and she's made Dad happy, which is the
main thing,' answered Fay, conscious that Lewis was
listening intently to this information. 'Yes, I think I *will*
go and see the New Year in with them,' she decided.

'One of these days you'll have a nice wee home and
family of your own, no doubt,' smiled the older midwife kindly, and a shadow passed over the doctor's face
at hearing these words.

At this moment one of the antenatal patients
appeared at the door in her dressing-gown.

'Excuse me, Sister Mitchell, I'm sorry to bother you,
but we're all ever so worried about young Jody
Pockett,' she said. 'She's in terrible pain, and says she
thinks the baby's coming early. Breaking her heart, she
is!'

Fay smiled and rose immediately.

'Oh, dear, poor Jody. I'll come to see her straight away. Thanks for letting me know, love.'

When she had gone to listen to Jody's latest tale of woe, Sister Pardoe shook her grey head.

'Mark my words, Dr Grant, one of these days the Pockett girl will "cry wolf" once too often, and have the baby in the bed!'

'Not if Sister Mitchell's on duty,' he corrected her firmly. 'She never runs out of patience—or pity.'

'I think maybe you're right, Doctor,' replied the Scotswoman, her pleasant, homely features softening. She liked the quiet anaesthetist, and wished him well.

When Fay arrived back at number thirty-seven at half-past nine that evening, her heart beat a little faster when Abigail met her in the front hall with the news that she, Fay, had a gentleman visitor.

'I've put him in the front parlour downstairs, Fay, so that you can have a private talk together,' she smiled. 'I'll brew up and bring in a tray for you.'

Fay was delighted to think that Lewis had taken up her invitation, and stepped into the parlour with a smile that froze on her face when Nicholas Lisle rose to greet her.

'Wherever do you hide yourself these days, Fay? I never get a moment alone with you—all right, all right, I'll keep my distance,' he said hastily, seeing her unwelcoming expression. 'I've brought you an important invitation.'

'I'm too busy for parties, Dr Lisle,' she told him firmly.

'Ah, but this one's different, Fay. This is a request from my mother for you to attend her dinner party on

New Year's Eve. I know that you can come, because I checked the duty roster.'

'I'm sorry, but I'm going to see my father at New Year,' she said.

'Now, Fay, just listen for a minute, will you? It's important. My father is putting a lot of money into the Lisle Birthing Clinic, and he and I will jointly interview and appoint the staff. Of course, I know exactly who I want for the senior positions, and this seems an ideal opportunity for you to meet my parents in a friendly social way. They're dying to see you, and—well, I'll be very proud to introduce you, Fay.'

There was an unusual note of pleading in his voice, and his blue eyes were anxious as he waited for her to speak. She gave a shrug of annoyance. Why on earth was he so persistent in the face of her coolness? And why was she so sure that she did not want a prestigious, lucrative and exciting career in partnership with this man? The majority of her friends would think her crazy to refuse.

'Nicholas, I'm sorry. You must think me very ungrateful, but I'm not the right person for the job you're offering.'

'Rubbish! You're ideal in every way—a superb midwife, kind and level-headed, and you stick to your own judgement, which I admire. Look, we won't argue if you're tired, but just tell me that you'll come to dinner on New Year's Eve. It doesn't commit you to anything. One of the guests will be Joanna Leach. You read her national newspaper column, don't you?'

'Joanna Leach?' repeated Fay, intrigued in spite of herself at hearing the name of the top journalist whose witty, wide-ranging comments and interviews were enjoyed by countless readers.

'Yes, the great Joanna herself. And guess what?

ARE YOU A FAN
OF MILLS & BOON
MEDICAL ROMANCES?

IF YOU are a regular United Kingdom buyer of Mills & Boon Medical Romances you might like to tell us your opinion of the books we publish to help us in publishing the books *you* like.

Mills & Boon have a Reader Panel of Medical Romance readers. Each person on the panel receives a questionnaire every third month asking her for *her* opinion of the past twelve Medical Romances. All people who send in their replies have a chance of winning a FREE year's supply of Medical Romances.

If YOU would like to be considered for inclusion on the Panel please give us details about yourself below. We can't guarantee that everyone will be on the panel but first come will be first considered. All postage will be free. Younger readers are particularly welcome.

Year of birth . . . . Month . . . .

Age at completion of full-time education . . . .

Single ☐ Married ☐ Widowed ☐ Divorced ☐

If any children at home, their ages please . . . .

Your name (print please) . . . .

Address . . . .

. . . .

. . . . Postcode . . . .

THANK YOU! PLEASE TEAR OUT AND POST
NO STAMP NEEDED IN THE U.K.

DR0992/RD

2

BUSINESS REPLY SERVICE
Licence No. SF195

MILLS & BOON READER PANEL
P.O. BOX 152,
SHEFFIELD S11 8TE

TAKE FOUR
BEST SELLER ROMANCES
FREE!

♥

Best Sellers are for the true romantic! These stories are our favourite Romance titles re-published by popular demand.

♥

And to introduce to you this superb series, we'll send you four Best Sellers absolutely FREE when you complete and return this card.

♥

We're so confident that you will enjoy Best Sellers that we'll also reserve a subscription for you to the Mills & Boon Reader Service, which means you could enjoy...

♥

Four new novels
sent direct to you every two months (before they're available in the shops).

Free postage and packing
we pay all the extras.

Free regular Newsletter
packed with special offers, competitions, author news and much, much more.

Mills & Boon FREE BOOKS CERTIFICATE

YES! Please send me my four **FREE** Best Sellers together with my **FREE** gifts. Please also reserve me a special Reader Service subscription. If I decide to subscribe, I shall receive four superb Best Sellers every other month for just £6.40 postage and packing free. If I decide not to subscribe I shall write to you within 10 days. Any **FREE** books and gifts will remain mine to keep. I understand that I am under no obligation whatsoever - I may cancel or suspend my subscription at any time simply by writing to you. *I am over 18 years of age.*

9A2B

MS/MRS/MISS/MR _____

ADDRESS _____

_____

POSTCODE _____ SIGNATURE _____

POST TODAY
and we'll send you this
cuddly Teddy Bear.

**PLUS a free
mystery gift!**
we all love mysteries, and
so we've an intriguing gift
especially for you.

MILLS & BOON
FREEPOST
P.O. BOX 236
CROYDON
CR9 9EL

She's booked for the birthing-room in February—first baby at thirty-nine, and absolutely over the moon. You and she will get along fine. How about it?'

'I'll let you know, Nicholas,' said Fay slowly.

'Oh, Fay, this is ridiculous!'

'I said I'll let you know—and now I must say goodnight, and go up to see Susannah.'

He was about to protest, but remembered the last occasion when he had tried to get the better of her, and gritted his teeth as he smiled and took his leave, just as Abigail brought in a tray of steaming coffee and gingerbread warm from the oven. Fay thanked her, and took the tray upstairs to share with Susannah; she also shared the news of the invitation to dine at the Lisles's on New Year's Eve.

'It would be such *fun* to dress up and go to a really classy dinner party, and hob-nob with Joanna Leach! Why don't I just accept and *go*?' she asked, hoping that her friend would persuade her.

'It depends on why you are hesitating,' replied Susannah wisely. 'Suppose Dr Grant asked you to *his* home on New Year's Eve, to meet *his* mother: would you need to ask my advice about which invitation you should accept?'

Fay stared in surprise for a moment, then shook her head, smiling at the other girl's perception.

'But he hasn't asked me,' she pointed out.

'So—will you go for the available option?' persisted Susannah.

'That makes it sound awful!' protested Fay.

And she thought of Matthew Okoje. Did Susannah look upon *him* as an available option? How complicated life was!

'I shall have to sleep on it,' she said finally. 'Tomorrow's going to be another busy day. I have to sort out the Christmas decorations for the antenatal ward, and Rachel Bamford's having an induction of labour. Her blood-pressure hasn't really settled, and Mr Horsfield's decided to get her delivered at thirty-nine weeks. She and her parents are going to need a lot of support. Oh, Susannah, thank heaven for our patients! They're so much easier to cope with than our own lives, aren't they?'

CHAPTER SEVEN

FAY was no closer to making a decision when she got up and walked to work the next morning. There were just four days to go until Christmas, and the maternity department was beginning to look festive, with multi-coloured paper garlands linking the lights in the wards and corridor, and golden bells suspended at intervals down the length of the main antenatal ward. The student midwives had sprayed glittering white powdery 'snow' on the window-panes, and Staff Nurse Laurie Moffatt had acquired a spray of fresh mistletoe which she taped firmly into place beneath the office clock.

After taking the report from the night staff, Fay went straight to Rachel Bamford, who was lying on her bed trying to read a magazine, but finding it hard to concentrate. Her eyes brightened at the sight of Fay.

'Oh, Sister Fay, I'm so glad to see you!' she cried, sitting up and tossing aside the magazine. 'I hardly slept a wink last night. That prostin thingummy that Dr Gillis put into me yesterday evening has given me the most horrid pains in my tummy! The induction won't be as bad as this, will it?'

Fay hid her feelings behind a bright smile. She was used to doing this, but sometimes she found it quite difficult to be truthful with her patients without frightening them. Nobody could foretell what sort of a labour any woman was going to have.

'The night's over now, Rachel, dear,' she said. 'Everything seems worse at night, doesn't it, lying awake imagining what's going to happen? Mr Rowan

will be here at nine o'clock to break your waters for
you. He's very gentle, and you'll feel the fluid draining
away from around the baby. Pretty soon after that your
contractions will begin, and you'll go into labour; your
baby will be born some time today, though it's too
early to make a guess at how long it will take.'

'Will I have to have a drip up?' asked the girl
anxiously.

'I expect so, dear, but that's nothing to worry about.
It means that we can give you plenty of water, salt and
sugar to keep up your strength, as you may not feel
like eating very much. And if your contractions aren't
very strong, we can put a hormone into the drip to
speed things up a bit.'

Fay spoke reassuringly, but the schoolgirl's face fell
and her mouth trembled.

'Oh, Sister Fay, if I'd known about all this, and the
worry that poor Mummy and Daddy have had because
of me, I'd never have—— Oh!'

And she burst into tears. Fay quickly drew the
curtains around the bed, and sat down on it to give
Rachel a hug.

'Hey, this won't do! I pride myself on having a happy
ward, so let's have a smile from you, young lady—
come on!' Rachel wiped her eyes and managed a
watery smile. 'That's better! Your mother's going to
phone in at about ten, isn't she?'

'Yes, she's offered to come in and sit with me when
I get the—the contractions, and when the baby's born.
I don't know whether I really want her to, Sister. It's
going to be so upsetting for her, isn't it? And you know
that I'm not going to see the baby because it's going to
be adopted. Will Mummy see it?'

Fay patted the girl's flushed cheek.

'Let's just see how everything goes, shall we,

Rachel?' she suggested. 'Don't let's plan too far ahead, but take each step as it comes. Let's see, now, did the night staff give you an early breakfast?'

'Yes, I had tea and toast terribly early, and then Night Sister gave me an enema and a hot bath. She put me into this huge nightgown—look at it, open all down the back, isn't it *awful*?' She forced another smile through her tears.

'Is this a private conversation, or can a friend join in?' asked a pleasant male voice on the other side of the curtain.

'Dr Grant! Oh, Dr Grant, please come and wish me luck!' begged Rachel, and Fay was a little taken aback when Lewis parted the curtain and was seized by the girl, who threw her arms around him in a bear-hug.

'I'm so glad you're on duty today, you and Sister Fay—you're both so nice!' she whispered to him. Over Rachel's shoulder the anaesthetist and the midwife exchanged a brief glance, and Fay's mouth curved upwards in a smile at his wryly amused expression. But I know how Rachel feels, she thought. Everything's better and warmer and safer when Lewis is around.

Fay transferred the girl to Stage-One Room B, where Mr David Rowan the senior obstetric registrar was expertly quick at rupturing the membranes. After the syntocinon drip had been commenced, Rachel began to get regular contractions which showed on the monitor as fairly strong at four-minute intervals by midday. Dr and Mrs Bamford arrived at one, but the GP could hardly bear the sight of his daughter in pain, and left very soon to make some house-calls. His wife sat down in the armchair beside Rachel's bed.

Fay went for her afternoon off, leaving Sister Pardoe in charge. She spent the winter afternoon writing a few last Christmas cards and wrapping up small gifts for each of her antenatal patients. When she returned at five, Rachel was making good progress and was free from pain, thanks to the epidural anaesthetic that Dr Grant had commenced during the afternoon. The girl was dozing, but Mrs Bamford looked worn out.

Sister Pardoe handed over to Sister Starr, who was on the evening shift for the consultant delivery unit.

'Cervix eight centimetres dilated, so she'll aye be delivered before the night staff come on,' reported the Scotswoman; her prediction proved correct, and at twenty minutes past eight Susannah rang the call-bell for Fay's assistance; the baby's head was born, but Susannah was having difficulty delivering the shoulders, which were rather too wide to pass easily through the schoolgirl's narrow pelvis.

'Bleep the paediatrician, will you, Fay?' muttered Susannah. 'I shall have to rotate the shoulders and do a little tugging here.'

Mrs Bamford went white with alarm and dismay. The paediatrician on call was busy in the children's ward, and Fay found herself automatically asking switchboard to bleep Dr Grant. It seemed only a matter of seconds before he flew into the delivery-room.

'I shall have to turn her over on to her side,' gasped Susannah, panting for breath. 'It might just increase the pelvic outlet enough to get these shoulders through.'

'Don't *you* do it, Susannah!' ordered Lewis, pushing her aside and lifting Rachel over on the bed; Mrs Bamford stifled a cry as Susannah then safely guided the baby's body through the birth canal, to be received on to the warm towel that Fay had spread out on the delivery bed.

'It's a boy,' breathed Mrs Bamford, covering her face with her hand.

'A boy? Oh, let me see him! Please!' cried the young mother.

'Darling, wait a minute,' pleaded Mrs Bamford, unable to check the tears that sprang to her eyes at the sight of the new-born human being, her own flesh and blood.

'Gently now,' soothed Susannah, looping the umbilical cord over her hand before clamping and cutting the vital lifeline; the baby lay pale and still on the towel, and made no sound.

'Is the paediatrician coming?' asked Susannah as Fay passed a thin plastic tube into the baby's throat, and, by vigorously sucking, withdrew a considerable amount of cloudy liquid into the mucus extractor. Once his air passages were cleared, the child gave a spasmodic gasp.

'Give him to me,' said Lewis, taking him from Fay's hands and placing him in the resuscitation cot that stood in the corner of the delivery-room. The precious seconds ticked by, and the midwives held their breath and prayed.

'Hi, there, young fella,' muttered Lewis. 'I think you could use a little oxygen. Fay, get me an intubation tube and connector. Good girl. Thanks.'

'Please let me hold him!' wailed Rachel, and Susannah whispered to her as stage three of labour was accomplished—the expulsion of the placenta and membranes.

As Lewis continued to pump life-giving oxygen directly into the tiny chest, the baby gasped again and flexed his arms and legs in a sudden movement. This was followed by another gasp and then a piercing cry. His skin turned rosily pink, and he gave a louder yell, kicking at Lewis's hands with sturdy feet. Then the room was filled with the sound of his lusty crying, and

Fay closed her eyes in a brief, heartfelt prayer of thanksgiving. Mrs Bamford began to sob.

'Thank God! Oh, thank you, Dr Grant, Sister Starr, Sister Mitchell, thank you, thank you!' She was unable to control the emotion kept so long in check.

'Let me see him!' came the insistent plea from Rachel, and Fay looked questioningly at Mrs Bamford.

'Let Rachel hold him if he's all right, Sister,' instructed the new grandmother in a low voice, and Fay took the now loudly howling infant from Lewis and placed him in his mother's arms. Rachel smiled at him adoringly.

'Right, I'll be off,' murmured Lewis under his breath, and flew from the scene as quickly as he had come upon it.

Susannah wiped the perspiration from her forehead with the back of her green-sleeved arm.

'Fay, love, could you go and put the kettle on and ask Beryl to make tea for everybody? And let Dr Bamford in—the poor man's been sitting in the waiting-room for nearly an hour.'

Fay hurried to tell the white-faced GP that his daughter was safely delivered, and escorted him to the delivery-room; he looked as if he had aged ten years in the course of the day, but he greeted his wife and daughter with a heartfelt kiss, and gently stroked the head of his vocal grandson, still clutched firmly in Rachel's arms.

Fay then went to the kitchen and plugged in the electric kettle. As she was setting a tray with cups and saucers, she suddenly paused in her task as a thought struck her: something prompted her to tiptoe quietly to the office door and peep inside. Lewis Grant was standing at the uncurtained window, staring out into the mid-winter darkness. As she stood looking at him, he turned round to face her, and she drew in a sharp breath: his face was as pale as Dr Bamford's, and his grey eyes were clouded with some private agony.

'Are you all right, Lewis?' asked Fay. 'Dear Lewis, you're not well! What's the matter?' Her voice was thin and full of fear, quite unlike her usual cheery tone.

'It's all right, I'm fine. A bit tired, perhaps. Sorry!' He made an effort to speak lightly as he saw the concern in her face. 'Just one of those moments—a memory—it's a tragic situation, isn't it? There's no really happy ending for that family, is there?' He spoke somewhat disjointedly. 'But at least the kid's OK. He'll be all right. Healthy. Undamaged.'

'Sit down, Lewis,' ordered Fay in alarm. 'You must be tired out. How long have you been on duty? Look, wait here and I'll bring you a cup of tea as soon as it's made. Please, Lewis.'

He did not sit down, but continued to stand and stare at her helplessly.

And then she went to him. She never quite knew how it happened, but they were standing together under the clock. Under Laurie Moffatt's little bunch of mistletoe. Fay could not remember which one of them made the first move—perhaps they had both moved in unison. Her arms were around his neck, his were clasped around her shoulders. His head bent down to hers, and she raised her mouth to his. Their kiss was sweeter than when the angry Batman had kissed her after the Hallowe'en party; tenderly, almost reverently, his lips pressed against her softly yielding mouth, and she gave herself into his yearning arms as if she had always belonged there—and yet it was no more than a moment as measured by the clock beneath which they stood.

In those brief seconds Fay looked into her own heart

and understood many things that she had only half
realised before: first, that she loved Lewis Grant and
no other. She wanted to share his life and all that
would be involved by so doing, for better or worse.
Second, and just as certain, was the knowledge that
Lewis loved her in return, and had probably done so
for some time: it was now undeniable. This kiss was
not for some remembered woman in his past, but for
herself alone. The joyful revelation thrilled through
every fibre of Fay's being, and as they drew apart she
looked up at him with radiance in her dark eyes.

'Lewis. . .dearest Lewis,' she whispered, searching
for the reflection of her own happiness in his face.

It was not there: the eyes that looked down at her
were filled with misgiving and self-reproach.

'I'm sorry, Fay, I have no right——'

She laid a finger on his lips.

'No apology this time, Lewis,' she said in a low
voice, returning his gaze. 'You love me. I know you
do. And it's all right, you see, because I——'

'No, Fay, no! You mustn't—you don't know. I can't
offer you anything but trouble and difficulty—something I refuse to share with you. You have your career,
your chance of happiness in life with a normal family,
your lovely personality—oh, my dear, this is no use to
you!'

He turned away from her and sat down at the desk,
leaning his head on his hands. She saw the silver-grey
hairs at his temples, and she was about to touch his
bowed shoulders when she recollected herself. She was
on duty, and supposed to be making tea for a newly
delivered patient and her relatives.

'Lewis, we can't talk now,' she told him sensibly and
firmly. 'You'll have to come and see me at thirty-seven
Grange Road where we can talk privately in Mrs

Leroy's front parlour! Give me a phone call and we'll arrange a time to suit us both. Now I must get on with brewing up for Rachel and her parents and Susannah and you and me—I don't know where Beryl's got to, but there's the paediatrician galloping up the corridor to see a baby who doesn't need his services, thanks to you!'

She returned to the kitchen, and when she emerged, carrying a large tray, Dr Grant had left the department, leaving no message.

Fay waited for the telephone call that never came, and when they next met on duty Lewis Grant determinedly avoided being alone with her; as the last few days before Christmas sped by, she had to face the fact that at the moment of revelation he had decided to renounce their love once and for all, for some reason of his own that he refused to tell her.

Fay found it very difficult to prepare for the Christmas festivities in hospital while feeling so humiliated, but she managed it with the help of her pride as a nurse and midwife; none of her patients guessed at her secret heartache.

CHAPTER EIGHT

THE morning of Christmas Eve dawned grey and drizzly, and although Fay was not on duty until one she got up with Susannah, who was on the early shift, to share a breakfast of grapefruit, toast and coffee. Not even the cosiness of their flat and the little Christmas tree twinkling in the front window of the living-room could banish the ache in Fay's heart, but she was now well practised in the midwife's art of hiding her own feelings behind a brightly deceptive smile as she poured out coffee; its delicious aroma rose from the steaming mugs, and there was nothing artificial about Susannah's smile as she looked up at her friend.

'It's the most exciting sensation, Fay,' she confided. 'Like a flicker of a finger deep, deep down inside me. I thought I felt it move yesterday, but I wasn't quite sure. This morning, when I woke up, there it was, quite unmistakable!'

They looked across the table at each other. Susannah's eyes no longer seemed haunted, but filled with wonder, and a tender softness; her tall figure was daily becoming fuller as she nourished the new life within her.

'It must be a wonderful feeling, Susannah, love,' replied Fay, thankful to see the change in her friend's attitude towards her pregnancy, now just halfway through. As long as she doesn't guess how un-Christmassy *I* feel, it won't be so bad, Fay told herself.

'Are you coming to Miss Clothier's coffee and mince pies in the school this morning?' asked Susannah. It was a Christmas Eve tradition that the senior midwife invited all her nursing staff and as many of the doctors as could take ten minutes off, to an elaborate 'elevenses' in the midwifery training school. It began at ten and went on till twelve, so that staff could take it in turns to attend.

'I don't know. I've got a few last presents to wrap up—and it will mean putting my uniform on, because there won't be time to come back to the flat afterwards,' said Fay unenthusiastically.

'Oh, do come, Fay—you can go straight to lunch in the canteen afterwards,' replied Susannah. 'Anyway, I must be off now, it's a quarter past seven—bye-bye, love!'

And, giving her friend the usual affectionate kiss, the Trinidadian girl hurried down the stairs.

Fay hastily completed the sewing-up of the little white cardigan she had knitted, with matching hat and mittens; wrapping it in tissue paper, and placing it in a decorated gift box, she wrote on the label, 'To our Baby, with love from Auntie Fay', and added it to the presents around the base of the tree. Taking a sheet of brightly coloured paper, she wrapped it round the handsome, brass-handled pot that held the crimson poinsettia she and Susannah had bought for Abigail Leroy.

By the time her tasks were completed, and the flat tidied, it was nearly eleven, and she decided to make the effort to go to Miss Clothier's coffee-morning. She changed into uniform, and put on her navy gabardine and black shoes. Walking briskly along Beltonshaw's main road, she tried hard to bring back the magic of Christmas to her heavy heart; but, in spite of all her natural bouncy optimism, she was plagued by unhappy thoughts.

Lewis Grant: she could hardly bear to think about him. Her cheeks burned at the memory of their kiss under the mistletoe, and how she had spoiled it by her impulsive declaration that he loved her—and she would have added that she loved him in return if he had not stopped her indiscreet, embarrassing tongue! She was thankful that he would soon be on his way home for Christmas, and doubted that he would put in an appearance at the coffee-morning.

Then there was Nicholas Lisle, who had hardly been able to believe his ears when she had told him that she would not be able to accept his mother's invitation to the New Year's Eve dinner party.

'Oh, for God's sake, darling, there's no need for you to be shy! I'll be there to introduce you, and the parents can't wait to meet this lovely girl I've told them about!' he protested in what she felt was a patronising attempt to reassure her.

Irritated by his obstinacy, she had replied sharply, 'I said *no*, Nicholas! Do you want me to write it down for you? I'm going to visit my father. How many more times do I have to tell you?'

'You can visit your father at any time!' he exploded. 'Can't you see that it's your future we're talking about?'

'And can't *you* understand that I'm not interested in a private clinic for privileged women?' she retorted.

'Look here, Fay, don't press your luck too far,' he threatened. 'There are plenty of other girls who would be glad to be asked!'

'Then why not ask them? There's Ann Clothier for one—she'd jump at the chance, I'm sure,' Fay had snapped back, though she was immediately ashamed of such a frankly catty remark.

She sighed now at the thought of their undignified exchange, and wondered if Lisle would be partaking of

Miss Clothier's coffee. She began to feel very reluctant to attend it after all.

And there was another sad thought: Rachel Bamford's Christmas this year would be shadowed. For the schoolgirl had surprised everybody, including Fay, by making a brave and unselfish decision, all by herself and without pressure from her parents. After holding her beautiful baby son in her arms, she had eventually kissed him and whispered, 'Goodbye, my little boy.' He was to go to foster parents for six weeks prior to being placed for adoption, as at first arranged. Everybody had been deeply sympathetic, from her sorrowful parents to Mr Horsfield, who had allowed her to go home on the day after her delivery because of the special circumstances.

Fay had kissed Rachel goodbye, also Mrs Bamford, and congratulated the young girl on her courage.

'Mrs McClennan will make sure that he goes to a really good couple who will bring him up well and give him more love and care than many a child gets from its natural parents,' Fay assured them truthfully, adding quietly to Mrs Bamford, 'Rachel will be able to go on studying for her A levels now, and I know she'll do well and go on to university. Everything will be all right, you'll see!'

'You're very kind, Sister Mitchell, but we can't turn the clock back,' replied Mrs Bamford sadly. 'Rachel has become a mother, and I shall always remember that I have a grandson somewhere in the world. Our lives have been changed, and can never be quite the same as they were before.'

Fay could not deny the truth of these words, but she wished Rachel success and happiness with all her heart.

Arriving at the hospital and making her way along the main corridor to the midwifery training school, she stopped outside the hospital chapel where there was a notice saying that there would be a midday Mass on Christmas Eve, and that Father Naylor the hospital chaplain was available to hear confessions beforehand. Fay thankfully decided to take advantage of this, gladly abandoning Miss Clothier's mince pie and cup of coffee with its festive addition of a teaspoonful of whisky. To remember the true message of Christmas will do me far more good, she thought as she entered the priest's little office and returned his friendly smile of greeting. As she sat down, he uttered the formal welcome, then waited for her to speak the words that only the priest might hear and never divulge.

When she had finished, his kindly face was very thoughtful. He counselled her to be patient, and try to forget her own problems in serving the mothers and babies in her care. Fay nodded, and bowed her head for the absolution.

But Father Naylor hesitated, and, leaning forward, he looked earnestly into her face, as if wanting to speak more particularly to her.

'Faith, my dear,' he said at last, using the name by which she had been baptised, 'it may be that there is a special work awaiting you, something that only you can take on. You may not know yet what it is, but may you be guided in the right direction, and find it! Live up to your name, Faith, and you will find your own happiness in giving it to those who need you, dear.'

He then said the absolution and gave her a blessing. Her thoughts were whirling as she took her place in the chapel, and saw Lewis Grant sitting two rows in front of her. She pondered over Father Naylor's words, which although rather mysterious were also strangely encouraging, and she was very glad that she had obeyed the impulse that had brought her to this place. When the small congregation gathered at the altar rail to receive the sacrament, she found herself kneeling beside the man she loved, and her heart swelled with a sudden joy in the shared moment of blessing, even though he hurried out of the chapel at the end of the Mass with only a brief handshake and a murmured, 'Happy Christmas, Fay.'

Her spirits had lifted by the time she went on duty after lunch in the canteen. Whatever set-backs might come her way, she resolved that her chief aim during this festive season must be to give her ladies-in-waiting as happy a Christmas as she possibly could.

Christmas morning in the maternity department was considerably enlivened by a visit from 'Woman of the Year' columnist Joanna Leach who wanted to write an on-the-spot account of Christmas at Beltonshaw General Hospital.

'I've just seen her going into the birthing-room with Miss Clothier and Nicholas Lisle, accompanied by a bearded individual with half a dozen cameras slung round his neck,' Dr Rose Gillis told Fay with a disapproving shrug. 'Isn't it ridiculous, a primigravida of her age, booking for the boudoir? I wonder at Mr Horsfield's allowing it.'

Fay smiled charitably. 'He knows she'll probably end up in the consultant delivery unit, anyway! Have you seen her column lately? Apparently she's going to do a weekly "diary" of her pregnancy from now on, ending with the delivery and the joys of breast-feeding.'

'Complete with photographs, no doubt!' added Laurie Moffatt. '*That'll* send the sales up, won't it? Frankly the whole thing makes me sick, all this fuss over one woman just because she's made a pile from writing a load of rubbish every week in a——'

'Sssh!' hissed Fay as they heard the sound of the lift doors banging and several pairs of footsteps coming along the corridor. She quickly straightened her cap and stood at the office door with the welcoming smile of a good hostess.

A very attractive, intelligent-looking woman with impeccable make-up and silver-blonde hair headed the group of approaching visitors. She wore a voluminous maternity dress in midnight-blue velvet with creamy lace at the throat and wrists, and she strode ahead of her followers who included Mr Horsfield, Dr Lisle and Miss Clothier, who gave Fay a sharp, self-satisfied look.

'Sister Mitchell! A very happy Christmas to you!' cried the beaming pregnant lady, holding out both her hands to Fay. 'I'm Joanna Leach, and this is my husband, Gordon Swayne. Meet my friend and photographer Roger here——' she waved her hand towards him '—and please introduce me to all your lovely nurses. Roger's dying to take pictures of you— yes, you too, Derek, even though you're so grumpy about Ann's beautiful birthing-room!'

Fay winced at hearing the consultant, Mr Horsfield, addressed as Derek, but joined in the general smiling and hand-shaking.

'Now I absolutely *insist* on meeting the poor dear mothers who are having to spend Christmas in hospital,' went on Joanna, and Fay accompanied her on a tour of the antenatal ward, where she spoke to every patient in turn and joked with them about her own bulging tummy, of which she was obviously proud. She then went to see the stage-one rooms, delivery-rooms and Theatre which made up the consultant delivery unit, accompanied by Sister Pardoe. It was impossible not to be amused by her extrovert manner, and Fay was impressed by her genuine interest in everybody she met.

'Isn't Derek Horsfield a perfectly *dear* old thing?' she said to Fay in a confiding whisper. 'Mind you, he's not a bit co-operative about my plan for a totally natural childbirth; in fact he's made me sign a tiresome piece of paper giving my consent to be transferred to that awe-inspiring delivery unit at any time during my labour. He says he won't be responsible for my care otherwise—he made it sound so terribly dramatic! Is he like that with all his patients?'

She chattered on in a light-hearted fashion as Roger's camera clicked and her husband placed a huge box of expensive chocolates on the office desk.

'Honestly, Fay, I feel much better now that I've met you and Sister Pardoe and all your staff. I shan't be half so scared if Derek insists on transferring me up here!' she declared as her party prepared to leave for coffee in Miss Clothier's office.

'Why, did she think we were all cross-eyed hunchbacks with warts on the end of our noses?' asked Laurie quietly, but just loud enough for the photographer to grin broadly in her direction as he caught the words.

'Well, at least she was nice to my patients and gave them something to tell their visitors this afternoon,' admitted Fay, popping a cherry liqueur chocolate into her mouth. 'I wonder if we'll all be in next week's "diary"?'

At half-past four that afternoon, when the patients and their visitors had all been served with sandwiches, savouries and Christmas cake, Fay found herself chatting with Matthew Okoje. He had just returned from taking Susannah home in his car, as Sister Pardoe had said she was looking tired and there were enough staff on to cope.

'Sister Starr is a different girl since you moved into Mrs Leroy's,' he remarked with satisfaction.

'Yes, it's such a relief to see her smiling again,' agreed Fay. 'And you're looking happier, too, Matthew. Who knows what the New Year will bring for us all? Have a salmon sandwich,' she added, pushing the plate across the office desk. 'Shall I make some more coffee?'

'Yes, please. Fay, I can never thank you for all you've done for her. Please let me tell you something— I don't suppose it will surprise you to know that I want to marry her.'

Fay hesitated. 'I'm not surprised, Matthew, but——'

'Oh, I wouldn't ask her in her present situation,' he assured her hastily. 'I couldn't bear it if she refused me! Fay—does she still hope that the—the artist will turn up again?'

'I don't think there's much chance now,' she replied candidly. 'I haven't seen so much as a Christmas card from him.'

'You never know, he just might come back after the child is born,' he went on. 'Everything will be different then, and I shall not lose any chance I may have! Will you be a friend to me, Fay? I intend to ask her as soon as she has recovered from the delivery. I want to be a father to the child, and give it my name, you see.'

His deep voice was very low, and Fay's eyes misted as she saw the love and devotion in his honest face. Impulsively she took hold of his hand.

'I'll do what I can to prepare the ground for you, Matthew. You're the best thing that ever happened to

Susannah,' she said huskily. 'Depend on it, I'll dance at your wedding before next Christmas!'

She turned away and looked out of the window at the lights of the suburban sprawl as Beltonshaw settled down to the evening of Christmas Day.

'Matthew, if I use my influence on your behalf, will you do something for me in return?'

'Anything, Fay! You have only to ask,' he replied.

'It's about Lewis Grant. Could you use your influence on *my* behalf?'

A shadow passed over his face.

'Ah, that isn't easy, Fay. There are problems and I'm not free to speak.'

She faced him levelly. 'I know that Lewis has some trouble, some burden that he doesn't want to share with me,' she said bluntly. 'Can you give me any idea of what's holding him back?'

'No, my dear. I've given my word.'

'Very well, Matthew—but I'll tell you this much, I'll find out for myself.'

'Then I just hope that neither of you will be hurt, Fay.'

'Sometimes I think we have to take the risk of being hurt, as you very well know,' she answered. 'I think I'm going to have to shake Lewis up a little, and make him realise that love can overcome problems, even heavy burdens, when it's strong enough.'

Matthew was silent, and looked at her determined little face as he turned over the thoughts in his mind.

'You're a strong woman, Fay,' he said at last, 'and you mean what you say. I'll give you one piece of information, but you must never say that you got it from me!'

'Guide's honour!' she replied eagerly. 'Tell me!'

'I'll write it down for you,' he said, taking a notebook

from the pocket of his white coat. He wrote a few words on a page which he tore out and handed to her.

'There, Fay! Do what you please with it!'

She looked at the scrap of paper and read:

> Pear Tree Cottage, Ively Lane, Barfylde, North Lancs.

For a moment she did not understand, but then she gave a whoop of joy.

'Is this his address? Where his mother lives?'

He nodded.

'Matthew, you've just solved the problem of how I shall spend the New Year! He's working, but I'm free to go on a rural hike in the wilds of north Lancashire!'

He smiled. 'I think you could describe it as fairly rural, yes.'

She leaned forward and kissed his cheek.

'Merry Christmas and Happy New Year, Matthew.'

When Dr Lisle looked into the antenatal ward a little later, he was taken aback by the sight of Fay capering hand-in-hand with Dr Okoje between the two rows of beds, a tinsel halo on her dark head in place of her cap, leading the patients and their visitors in a harmonious chorus:

'Glor—i—a! In excelsis Deo!'

Lisle's handsome face was unsmiling. Yes, he thought, she's doing her best to try me out, playing hard to get, wanting me to sit up and beg! But I'm calling your bluff this time, you little witch, and I wonder how you'll feel when you hear that I've asked Ann Clothier to come to my mother's dinner party?

And so Christmas Day came to an end for another year, and most of the maternity staff agreed that it had been a happy time. Miss Clothier was frantically going through her wardrobe, looking at her dresses, shoes and jewellery, and deciding that she would have to buy a completely new outfit before New Year's Eve. She could scarcely believe her luck: *this* was an unmistakable move on the part of dear Nicholas. . .and what a slap in the face for that impertinent Sister Mitchell!

Fay's resolution strengthened during the days following Christmas: she was convinced that her love for Lewis—and her certainty that he also loved her—could overcome all obstacles. She would go on a secret expedition to his home, to meet his mother and make a friend of her if at all possible. The two full days' leave she would have over the New Year, knowing that Lewis would be on call for the whole of that period, now appeared to be a heaven-sent opportunity to find out for herself what Lewis so adamantly refused to share with her. May you be guided in the right direction, Faith! Father Naylor's words now seemed to have a clear meaning, and she was determined that she would indeed live up to her name.

She had only occasional glimpses of Lewis after he returned to Beltonshaw on Boxing Day, and he continued to keep his distance. Once, when Sister Pardoe asked him within Fay's hearing if he had found his mother well, he replied briefly that everything at home was fine, and that he had enjoyed being there for Christmas. Now that Fay had made up her mind what she intended to do, she was able to relax more when they met, and return his cool, professional tones with a polite smile.

The last remaining days of the year passed slowly by, and the morning of New Year's Eve dawned, grey and wet. Fay rose early, having sorted out the hiking gear that she had worn in the Lake District the previous year. An extra sweater and a flask of coffee were packed in a rucksack, and as she stood on the railway station platform wearing a blue anorak, matching waterproof leggings over her trousers, hiking boots and a knitted wool hat over her mop of curls she felt ready to face whatever adventures the day might bring. The train would take her to within twelve miles of Barfylde, and from there she would go on a cross-country hike guided by her ordnance survey map.

She had told Abigail that she was joining a rambling party for the New Year, but the one person she could not deceive was of course Susannah.

'You don't have to tell me anything, Fay, love,' her friend had said gently. 'Just take good care of yourself in this winter weather, and come back safely. And I hope you will find what you are looking for!'

Fay had smiled and said nothing. There was an unspoken understanding between the two of them, although Fay had not told of her love for Lewis, nor had Susannah mentioned Matthew.

Once she was in the train, leaving Manchester and its industrial suburbs behind, the rolling Lancashire countryside looked very bleak: bare moors, slate quarries and disused textile mills passed by the carriage window under a lowering sky from which grey curtains of rain swept across the distant hills. Fay had to stop herself from giving way to niggling doubts and misgivings: she was going after what she most wanted in life—the man she loved. It had taken her a long time to realise that Lewis Grant was the only man for her, and she believed that she could make him happy if he would only allow her to try. She needed to get to know about him, to find out his background; she wanted to share his life, and therefore his secrets were her concern, or would become so. His family would be her family, his burdens would be hers to share. She held up her firm little chin and resolved that nothing would stand in her way: she would accomplish what she had set out to do, even though she did not know what she would discover while Lewis was on duty at Beltonshaw General over this New Year.

She got off the train at a small industrial town that looked very dismal in the pouring rain. Walking across a cobbled square to an almost deserted bus depot, she found that there would not be a service bus in the Barfylde direction for three hours, so resigned herself to a very wet walk. It was time for coffee, she decided, and as she sat on a damp wooden seat and struggled with the fastenings of her rucksack a gleaming estate car drew up on the road near by, and the passenger door opened invitingly.

'Sister Mitchell! It *is* you, isn't it?' Fay looked up in surprise to see a man in a well-cut suit at the steering-wheel, and a woman with a two-month-old baby in the back seat. 'Sister Mitchell! Can we offer you a lift?' called the man with a smile.

Fay got up and advanced to the car, racking her brains to put a name to the couple. She knew she had seen them before.

'What a nice surprise, Sister!' exclaimed the woman. 'How are you? And how is that wonderful Dr Grant who took away the pain that *this* young man caused me?' She proudly indicated her baby boy, and at once Fay remembered them. Mr and Mrs Forbes, of course! Irene Forbes who had had to wait so long for her epidural.

'Hello! Yes, *what* a surprise!' she responded, hoping desperately that they were going in her direction. 'And doesn't Baby look fine?'

'Jonathan Forbes junior!' beamed his mother. 'Look, he's smiling at you!'

'Where are you going on this wet New Year's Eve, Sister?' asked Mr Forbes.

'I'm hoping to find my way to visit some people in Barfylde, actually,' replied Fay, crossing her fingers inside her mittens.

'In you get, then! We're on our way to spend New Year with Irene's parents at Carnforth, but we can take you to within about five miles. It's a pleasure,' Mr Forbes assured her.

Thankfully Fay edged into the passenger-seat, and stowed the rucksack in the capacious area at the back. The car zoomed away, and she chatted pleasantly with the Forbes couple while inwardly exulting over such a marvellous coincidence. Surely she must be meant to go to Barfylde! It never occurred to her that it was anything to do with her kindness and patience at the time of Irene's labour that they had recognised her with enough gratitude to stop and give her a lift.

The car halted at a lonely crossroads near to an ancient village church.

'There you are, Fay,' said Mr Forbes. 'Take the road up past that church, and after about two miles you'll come to a pub where there should be a signpost to Barfylde. We'd take you the whole way, only we're already a bit late. Happy New Year—and thanks for everything!'

'You, too!' called Fay gratefully, hoisting her ruck-sack on her shoulders and waving after the car as it disappeared out of sight.

The rain had eased a little, but the walk was longer and harder than she had expected, and she could not find the signpost to Barfylde until she had tramped for miles along narrow, winding lanes between forlorn wet fields. When at last she approached a huddled group of slate-roofed cottages and a little general store with

'Barfylde Post Office' above the door, she was alarmed to see that the winter daylight was already fading over the bare fields and leafless trees. Tired, wet, hungry and cold, she entered the post office and asked for directions to Ively Lane.

'It's a tidy way out o' t' village, love,' said the sub-postmistress, coming out from behind the counter and standing at the doorway to point towards a straggling unpaved track.

Fay thanked her, and bought a bar of chocolate. Heaving up her rucksack again, she set off uphill for about half a mile, over a dripping tree-crowned summit and down a stony pathway to where a single cottage stood outlined against the darkening sky. A freak gust of wind tore the wool hat from her head and flung it into a thorny bush; she retrieved it and plodded on through the drizzle towards the cottage. It was solidly built with leaded windows and blue-grey slate tiles, and the date '1881' was carved in stone above the arch of the door. There was a faint light shining through from the back of the house, but no other sign of life.

Fay now experienced the first chill of dismay as she hesitated at the gate of this stark and solitary house. It was the most isolated spot she could have imagined. She wondered with sudden panic how Lewis's mother would react to a total stranger who came knocking on the door at such a time. Will she just turn me away and shut it in my face? she asked herself. And if so, what shall I do?

Her journey to this lonely house now seemed to be the limit of absurdity. What right had she got, anyway, to come intruding into heaven only knew what dark secret of Lewis's life? Her teeth began to chatter with cold, and she realised that she was wet through.

You must live up to your name, Faith! Once again

she recalled the words of Father Naylor. She whispered
a little prayer, and then summoned up all her courage
and determination, all the persuasive charm and wit
that had made her one of the most popular nurses at
Beltonshaw General. Walking boldly up to the front
door, she tapped three times with the heavy brass
knocker. There was no reply, and she was about to
knock again when a child's clear voice piped up behind
the door.

'Will you please come round to the back door? I
can't open this one!'

'Right-oh!' called out Fay as cheerfully as she could,
and walked round the side of the house to a paved
backyard where there was a lighted window and
another solid-looking door. A black cat ran up to the
stone step as soon as she saw Fay approach, and Fay
bent down to give her a quick stroke for luck.

A key turned in the lock, and the door was pulled
back. And then Fay was confronted with a solemn-
faced boy who stared at her from the doorway. He
seemed to be about eleven or twelve years old and had
large, innocent grey eyes and dark, wavy hair. Fay
particularly noticed his small, neat ears set close against
his head—and her heart gave a leap: this could be
Lewis Grant as a young boy. She smiled at him, and
felt a tremendous sense of warmth when he smiled
back at her and spoke with a straightforward
familiarity.

'Hello! I'm Tommy Grant, and this cat's name is Mrs
Black. We've got another one called Podger, and a
little one that Daddy calls the Dreaded Piddler.'

'Hello, Tommy. I'm so pleased to meet you. I'm
F-Faith.'

'You've got a very nice face, Faith,' he told her.
'Doesn't that sound funny?'

And they both laughed, though inwardly Fay was in a turmoil. She remembered when she had first met Dr Lewis Grant: he had made little impression on her at the time, and it had taken quite a while for her to realise gradually that she loved the man and believed that he loved her in return; but on this first meeting with his son it was a case of love at first sight. On both sides. She was immediately aware that this was a very special child, and felt protective towards him, forgetting her own apprehension.

'Will you come into the kitchen, Faith, and wait for Granny? She's out putting the chickens to bed, but she'll be in soon.'

So Fay stepped over the threshold of Pear Tree Cottage and followed Tommy, who dragged his left leg slightly, turning the foot inwards. Mrs Black the cat trotted along with them into a large, old-fashioned kitchen filled with warmth and homeliness. A range oven gave out a delicious aroma of cooking, and a substantial table with four square-backed chairs was laid ready for a meal for two. Against one wall stood a fine Welsh dresser in dark hand-carved wood, displaying a willow-pattern dinner service and a row of cups suspended from brass hooks, while on the opposite side a long bench seat was piled with cushions, a sewing-basket, paint-box, sketching pad and a large grey tabby cat asleep on a crocheted shawl.

Fay blinked at the contrast between the cold, wet darkness outside and this haven of cosy comfort. How thankful Lewis must be to get back here, she thought at once—and in a strange way she felt that she too had arrived home. She had reached her journey's end, and as she took hold of Tommy's trusting hand she knew that she had come face to face with her destiny.

For this boy was a Peter Pan who would never grow

up: his body might be twelve years old, but he spoke and behaved like a friendly, well-behaved child of about seven. The term 'mentally retarded' came to Fay's mind, but it did not seem at all appropriate for this confiding little fellow who was so quickly claiming her heart. How could Lewis regard him as a burden, a secret trouble to be kept from her knowledge? She saw now all too clearly the explanation of Lewis's reservations about natural childbirth, for here was a child injured by birth—brain-damaged and with a spastic condition of his left leg. And his mother must have died. . . Fay caught her breath at the sadness of it.

'Tommy! What's to do? Lord save us! What are you about, lad, letting a stranger into t' house?'

And into the kitchen marched a dark-browed woman in her sixties, with a rather bony figure and deep lines around her eyes and mouth where time and trouble had left their mark. Again Fay noticed a resemblance to Lewis, but, unlike Tommy, the woman stared unwelcomingly at her.

'I'm very sorry, Mrs Grant, I shouldn't have come into your home without your permission,' began Fay pleadingly, still clutching Tommy's hand. 'I—I've got lost, and I wonder if you could let me have a cup of tea? I'll pay you, of course, and if I could just have a rest for a while, I——'

Suddenly she closed her eyes and sat down heavily on one of the kitchen chairs. Tears spilled down her cheeks and rain-water dripped from her clothes on to the red-tiled floor.

'Eh, now, lass, you look fair starved! What's your name? Happen you know mine already,' said the woman in a slightly softer tone.

'She's called Faith, and I like her a lot, Granny!' interposed Tommy.

'Faith? I had an aunt by that name, who went and married t' village blacksmith,' remarked his grandmother with a nod. 'You're not planning to walk further tonight, are you, lass?'

Fay shook her head.

'She can sleep in Daddy's room!' cried Tommy.

'Steady on, lad. Happen you'd best get out o' those wet clothes, Faith, and I'll put t' kettle on,' said Mrs Grant with sudden decision. 'I'll not ask why a young lass should be wandering around in these parts at this hour o' day and time o' year, but you're welcome to stay overnight in our Lewis's room if you want. He's my son, a doctor and mostly away, more's the pity.'

Fay felt even more certain that she had been guided to this place, and her emotions whirled.

'That's very good of you,' she managed to say shakily as she took off her anorak and waterproof leggings. Mrs Grant took them and hung them up to dry on an ancient airing-rack with a pulley that hoisted them up above the range oven.

'I pride myself on my judgement of character,' said the north-country housewife briskly, 'and our Tommy's taken after me that way. Besides which I wouldn't turn a dog away from t' door on a night like this, and folks say that a stranger over t' doorstep at New Year brings good luck into a house. I've a beef casserole in t' oven, and happen there's enough for three.'

Seated at the kitchen table in front of a steaming plate of meat and vegetables, Fay felt herself reviving, and answered her hostess's questions about her destination.

'I'm hoping to get down as far as Manchester tomorrow,' she said. 'I've got friends living there.'

'Oh, aye? My son works at a hospital not far out o'

t' city, at a place called Beltonshaw,' said Mrs Grant
with interest.

'Yes, Daddy puts people to sleep and then they don't
feel any pain,' added Tommy. 'And he came home for
Christmas and we went to church and had presents and
Christmas pudding and crackers and Daddy took us in
the car to see Auntie Jenny!'

'Stop and take a breath, our Tommy,' smiled his
grandmother. 'Aye, it were great this year, having
Lewis home for Christmas for once. Best time we've
had in years, and nice for t' poor little lad—he doesn't
see too much of his dad.'

Fay heard the tenderness in her voice, and felt drawn
towards this forthright woman who was the mother of
the man she loved.

'Does Tommy go to school?' she asked quietly.

'Aye, to t' convent yonder. The sisters let him stay
on, even though he's nearly thirteen and well past their
age limit for boys. It's better than having him go to
some special place a long way off. I like to have him
safe at home wi' me. He's a good boy, is our Tommy—
aren't you, lad?' she said fondly, her gaunt features
softening as she patted his head.

'Yes, I can draw and paint pictures of Mrs Black and
Podger and the Dreaded Piddler!' Tommy told Fay
eagerly.

'Steady, lad, you mustn't say that word to Faith,'
said Mrs Grant. 'He's talking about the cats, you see—
worships them, he does. Show Faith some of your
pictures, Tommy. They're really quite clever—at least
I think so.'

There was a note of pride in her voice, and Fay
smiled indulgently when Tommy brought his sketch-
book to the table. However, she stared in frank astonishment at the vigorous originality of the drawings and

water-colours, which seemed to catch the unique feline nature of the three cats: Mrs Black, neat-footed and short-haired; Podger who was fat but dignified, in contrast to Tinker, a green-eyed little rusty black chap who soon introduced himself to Fay in person, jumping on her lap and purring loudly.

'Daddy found him sinking in the pond, and pulled him out and brought him home to live with us,' explained Tommy. 'Granny calls him Tinker, but Daddy says he's the Dreaded Piddler because he goes upstairs and——'

'That'll do, lad,' interrupted Mrs Grant. 'Happen the poor creature had a bad time before he came to us, and we've never got him properly house-trained.'

Fay stroked the friendly little half-grown tom with amused sympathy as she admired Tommy's work.

'But these are *good*!' she declared. 'May I have one, Tommy? I'd like to frame it and hang it up in my room. Can I take this one of the Dreaded Pid—of Tinker?'

Tommy was delighted at her praise, and gave her half a dozen pictures. They showed a primitive talent that Fay felt might be marketable, and she wondered who she could ask for an expert opinion. It would be so good for Tommy if he could earn a little income of his own, she thought, and secretly questioned the policy of keeping him so sheltered from the world. She remembered the training college in Manchester where the mentally handicapped were helped to achieve their maximum potential in the special workshops, gymnasium and swimming-pool. What did the future hold for Tommy after his grandmother was gone? Mrs Grant was not young. Would he be put into some sort of institution? Not if I have any say in the matter, she thought suddenly: *I* shall look after Tommy when Lewis and I are married. Her heart leapt at the thought, and she and the boy exchanged a very special, loving look.

Tommy went to bed at half-past nine, and asked Fay to come and give him a goodnight kiss. His grandmother put out clean underwear, shirt and socks for the next day, and Fay saw herself taking on these duties in the happy future—how willingly she would become Tommy's new mother!

'Happen neither of us'll care to stay up to see another year in,' commented Mrs Grant when they returned to the kitchen, 'though I'll not deny that it's good to have company. We'll take a glass of sherry together, lass.'

'Oh, yes, Mrs Grant, and let's wish each other a *very* happy New Year!' cried Fay, knowing how deeply she meant it.

'My name's Mollie—well, it's Amelia really, but I've always been called Mollie, so never mind about "Mrs Grant",' smiled the older woman. 'And now I reckon it's time you told me about yourself, Faith. Where have you come from, lass, and what's your family name?'

Fay's heart lurched, and she lowered her eyes. What was she to reply? If she gave her name to Lewis's mother, he would soon hear of her visit, and she did not want him to know about it until she could tell him herself. For the time being she must conceal her identity, and yet she recoiled from telling a downright lie. Her full name was Faith Marsden Mitchell, and she decided on the spur of the moment not to give her surname.

'I'm Faith Marsden,' she said a little awkwardly. 'My father's home is at Nethersedge in Westmorland.'

'Oh, aye,' replied Mollie. 'That's Kendal way, so you've travelled quite a distance all on your own. What do your parents think of the way you spend New Year, then?'

'My father doesn't mind, he's a keen hiker himself, and my—my stepmother knows that I'm visiting friends in the Manchester area——' Fay hesitated, and Mollie gave a knowing nod.

'Ah, you've a stepmother, then. Happen you'd be spending New Year at home otherwise.'

'No, no, she's very nice,' protested Fay in embarrassment.

'Maybe so, but you're a young wee lass to be wandering around alone at such a time. I can see you're not above twenty years, if that. Have you a job?'

Fay had worked in a children's day nursery between leaving school and commencing nursing training, so without contradicting Mollie's assessment of her age she went back to those days.

'Yes, in a day nursery. I like children.'

'I can see that, lass. Well, I won't ask a lot of questions, Faith, your business isn't mine, but our Tommy's taken a fancy to you, and I'm grateful. You've brightened up the lad—he misses his father.' She sighed, and Fay hastily took this opportunity to change the subject.

'Did you say that your son is working tonight, Mollie?' she asked conversationally.

'Aye, he is that. And t' casualty department'll keep him busy, I dare say! Though happen he might get away to t' maternity ward, which may or may not be a good thing,' added Mollie quietly, as if talking to herself.

'Why do you say that, Mollie?' Fay enquired with sudden alertness.

The older woman shrugged.

'To be truthful, I think there's a midwife who's rather caught his eye. A sister, very efficient at her work—one of these career women. Not good for my son.'

There was a pause, and Fay's heart pounded, for she suspected that she herself could be the sister. She took a breath, and asked as casually as she could, 'If the midwife is as attached to your son as you think he might be to her, Mollie, why shouldn't they——?'

'My son's business is not for idle tittle-tattle,' interrupted Lewis's mother with unexpected sharpness. 'What does a young lass like you know what he's been through over our Tommy? Nay, don't look so taken aback, love. Happen I still can't bring myself to speak of it, even now. Eh, come and greet t' New Year wi' me!'

She took a plate of warmed mince pies out of the oven, and opened a bottle of home-made pear wine, pouring out two glasses of the sweet, rather heady liquid, halfway between a wine and a liqueur. The two women smiled at each other as they raised their glasses and clinked them together.

'To your folks and mine, Faith!'

'To our families and friends, Mollie!'

And they kissed each other goodnight.

As Fay lay in Lewis's bed and stared at the night sky through the window, joy and thanksgiving filled every fibre of her body; she could not sleep for sheer happiness as she planned what she would say to Lewis. She regretted the need to deceive Mollie Grant, but would beg to be forgiven as soon as she had confessed to Lewis and declared her love for both him and Tommy.

She pictured Lewis lying here in this room as a serious-faced schoolboy and idealistic teenager; then as a medical student, gradually broadening his horizons and visiting his childhood home at intervals. She found it hard to imagine the next phase: falling in love, marrying and becoming a father. . .and losing a wife. Fay shuddered at such bitter sorrow, and the tragedy of a brain-damaged child whose whole life was shadowed because of oxygen deprivation at the vital moment of birth. She thought of the effect it had had on Lewis, his withdrawal from close relationships, his gravity and occasional cynicism—and yet she rejoiced at the memory of those moments when his love for her had overcome his reticence, and he had held her briefly in his arms. Now his cryptic words were explained, and soon she would be in his arms again, telling him that he no longer had a secret burden, because she knew— *she knew!*—and would share Tommy with him so gladly. She glowed with anticipation.

In her happiness she spared a few thoughts for Ann Clothier at the New Year's Eve dinner party at the Lisles's, and wondered if Nicholas was being an attentive partner. She generously hoped that the senior midwife was enjoying herself, though she would not have changed places with her for anything.

Oh, happy, *happy* New Year, thought Fay joyously as she snuggled under the eiderdown where he had so often lain, and nestled against the pillow that had supported his dark head in good times and bad. I'll make him happy again, she resolved, and do all I can for Tommy. She smiled to herself: maybe Tommy would even get a baby brother or sister one of these days!

And, happier than she had ever been in her life before, Faith Marsden Mitchell fell at last into a deep, blissful sleep.

The skies cleared overnight, and Fay awoke to a cold, bright morning. For a half-second she wondered where she was, and then remembered. She closed her eyes and lay back on her bed, smiling as the happiness of last night flooded back into her heart. She then sat up and hugged her knees. Oh, what would Lewis say if he could see her now, at his home, in his bed? She longed to see him, to tell him, to share her New Year experience with him, and watch his astonishment turn to joy to match her own!

She glanced at her wristwatch: it was nearly half-past eight. As she got out of bed to go to the bathroom, she heard the telephone ring in the hall below, and Mollie going to answer it. Tiptoeing softly out to the landing at the top of the stairs, Fay heard Mollie speaking.

'No need to worry, I tell you! Can't you trust your mam's judgement by now? Yes, barely twenty, a tidy little body and very good with our Tommy—works in a children's nursery.'

There was a pause while Fay stood absolutely still, not daring to move in case a floorboard creaked. She held her breath while she waited for Mollie to resume talking.

'Oh, come off it, son. I'd give this little lass bed and board any time. Listen, Lewis, I'll tell you what made up my mind. It were the way our Tommy took to her, and she to him. Yes, I know, but this lass is different, she genuinely likes his company, and—wait, let me tell you! You know those sketches he does of the cats?'

'Granny! Let me speak to Daddy! Please!' came an excited voice as Tommy burst out of his room and almost collided with Fay on the landing.

'Careful, lad!' Mollie called up the stairs. 'Put your dressing-gown and slippers on first. It's fair perishing this morning.'

'Come downstairs, Faith, and say hello to Daddy with me!' cried the eager boy.

'Oh, *no*, Tommy, I must get dressed!' gasped Fay,

hastily returning to her room—*his* room—and closing the door behind her.

Presently Mollie came in with a mug of tea.

'The lad said you were up,' she smiled. 'I hope the telephone didn't wake you.'

'No, I was already awake, Mollie. Oh, thank you,' said Fay, gratefully warming her hands on the mug as she sipped the steaming brew. 'Happy New Year again!'

'It were my son, ringing up to say the same thing,' said Mollie, sitting down on the bed. 'He were right taken aback when I told him I'd a lodger overnight!'

Fay had already gained the impression that Lewis had been surprised and not too pleased to hear that his mother had allowed a complete stranger into the house—a stray girl hiker who was occupying his bed! Fay could not help being amused at the irony of the situation.

'Any road, our Tommy was full o' talk about you as soon as he got hold of the phone, so there was an end to it,' said Mollie. 'Now, what would you like for breakfast? I've got some eggs from my own chickens. It's not the best time o' year for laying, but there's ten o' them and I pick up two or three each day, even in winter.'

Fay aimed to leave by eleven and hike across country to reach Carnforth by mid-afternoon; from there she could catch a Manchester train, one of the very few running on the bank holiday. After she had breakfasted in the kitchen, there was time for her to yield to Tommy's entreaties to go out for a walk with him, and see the village by daylight.

Leaving Mollie feeding the chickens and preparing a packed lunch for her guest, Fay and Tommy walked hand in hand up Ively Lane to the high point she had come over the evening before in darkness and rain. In the clear light of the morning she stared around her in delight at a vista of fields and moorland with trees dotted here and there, the church spires of villages pointing up to the blue sky, and the outline of industry on the distant horizon. It was an unspoiled rural area where grazing land and ancient boundaries had survived industrial development. Even in the depths of winter, with leafless trees and thorny hedges, the place had an austere beauty that made Fay want to explore its history and get as closely acquainted with it as Lewis must be.

The post office and the few little shops were closed, but some villagers were about, and Tommy exchanged New Year greetings with everybody they met; the friendly local people all had a special smile and a word for him. He walked quite quickly in spite of his twisted left leg, and pointed out his school to Fay, a high-walled convent where one of the sisters appeared in the driveway and waved to them. It was obvious that Tommy was completely accepted by the village and used to receiving plenty of attention, but Fay still felt that he ought to be seeing more of life, meeting more people and learning to play his part in the world as far as he was able. I'll teach him to take care of himself, she decided, to wash his own socks and underwear, prepare simple meals and make his bed. She smiled happily to herself as she made her plans.

'Why are you smiling, Faith?' he asked innocently.

'I was just thinking how nice it is for us to be friends, Tommy.'

'Yes! We *are* friends, aren't we, Faith?'

'And we'll *stay* friends, Tommy!' She gave his hand a squeeze.

When they returned to the cottage, Mollie had

packed Fay's rucksack with sandwiches, cake and fruit, and refilled the coffee-flask. Fay sat down at the kitchen table while Tommy ran upstairs to the bathroom.

'It's been the best New Year ever,' she told Mollie truthfully.

'And it's been a right treat to have you here, Faith, and no mistake,' replied her hostess. 'You've made our Tommy's New Year, just as his daddy made his Christmas by being with us. I hope you'll find your way here again—and go ahead with that nurse training. You'll be champion, especially with children!'

Fay glowed with pleasure, and was strongly tempted to confess all to her future mother-in-law. She promised to keep in touch, and wrote out her father's address in Nethersedge, near Kendal.

'Mollie, I've got a feeling that this year really is going to be a good one for you and Tommy—and his father,' she confided. 'You do such a wonderful job taking care of Tommy, seeing that his mother. . .' Fay hesitated, then went on, 'I mean that her death must have been such a terrible. . .'

And again Fay faltered and stopped speaking as she saw the change in Mollie Grant's expression: the hardening of her stony grey eyes, and a bitter tightening of her mouth that made Fay recoil in shocked surprise.

'I'm afraid you've got it wrong where *that* one's concerned, Faith,' Mollie snapped. 'The boy's mother's not dead. She just deserted them, just upped and left the two who most needed her.'

'W-what?' Fay gasped slowly as she took in the meaning of the words.

'Aye, she's got somebody else now. We don't ever talk of her in front of Tommy, or even between ourselves now. God knows, my son has suffered for that woman, and still can't forgive himself for everything that happened. Blames himself for not being firmer over her crackpot ideas about giving birth. But oh, *I* shan't ever forgive her—never!'

'Oh, my God. . .oh, poor Lewis,' breathed Fay, and Mollie saw how white the girl's face had turned.

'Eh, lass, I shouldn't have upset you, it's not your fault. Let's have another cup o' tea, Faith, and we'll not speak of it again.'

But Fay had to pursue this latest bombshell.

'How long is it since she—left?' she asked, her voice thin and wavering. 'Please tell me, Mollie. I want to know.'

'What's it to you, Faith? The little lad were coming up to three years old, and we could see he were backward, like—and his foot were much worse then, he didn't walk till gone two years, and then only with calipers to straighten his leg. Lewis did all he could to help her and never reproached her, but it were no good. *She* were no good, Faith, as I could see from the start. Don't be sad about it—happen the boy's better off wi'out her.'

Mollie Grant's mouth tightened into a hard, straight line as she spoke, and Fay felt that a great black cloud had descended over the happiness of less than five minutes ago.

Lewis had a wife living. A numb dismay filled Fay's heart as the implications of this fact dawned upon her. His wife might have found another man, but he was still bound by his marriage vows and could not marry Fay or anybody else. He might even be clinging to a secret hope that Tommy's mother would return to them one day. . .

So *that* was the real reason for his behaviour: he was

simply not free to ask her to share his life, and she could never be a mother to his son. What a cruel blow, what an end to all her hopes and plans! She was too devastated for tears, and when Tommy came back into the kitchen she needed her courage and acting ability more than ever before in her life.

She rose to the occasion, smiling brightly as Tommy played with the indolent Podger, who rolled over on to his back in purring ecstasy. Fay yearned with tenderness at the sight of the boy's innocent romping, his extraordinary understanding of feline psychology; she thought of the remarkable studies of cats that he had sketched, and made up her mind that she would still make enquiries about finding a market for them. But she could not visit Barfylde again. It would be unwise, and could only lead to embarrassment all round when her identity was revealed, as would inevitably happen. At least Lewis would never know about this one and only expedition to his home.

Fay did not know how she brought herself to say goodbye to Tommy, who put his arms around her neck and begged her to come and see him again soon.

'One day, perhaps, Tommy——' She could not speak further, and Mollie gave her a look of concern.

'What's to do, Faith? Are you ill, lass? You'd better stay here—you don't look fit to hike all t' way to Carnforth!'

'I'm perfectly all right, Mollie,' Fay managed to affirm, once again hoisting the rucksack on her shoulders. 'I'll send Tommy a postcard, and thank you for all your. . .'

Her words tailed off as she almost ran up Ively Lane, not looking back, going over the summit that soon hid her from their sight.

As she plodded her way across the winter countryside, her thoughts whirled round and round in her head like a treadmill endlessly turning and finding no way out of the tragedy. There was no future in loving a married man who obviously did not want to be divorced. So much for her imagined happiness: the dream of love had turned into a nightmare of disappointment, and Fay reflected bitterly that if she had not gone on this ill-fated New Year expedition she would never have found out how deep was her loss. Not only must she give up Lewis, but Tommy, too, the boy she had so quickly befriended, and must now desert, just as his mother had deserted him. How could fate be so heartless?

It was dark when at last her train pulled in at the Manchester terminus. She felt mentally and physically exhausted as she stepped stiffly down on to the platform. Every part of her body ached, and all she wanted now was the privacy of her room at number thirty-seven Grange Road. She telephoned for a taxi to Beltonshaw, and during the drive she decided to tell no one about her New Year hike. She had just been for an away-from-it-all-break, staying at a remote bed-and-breakfast place where the food had been good and the weather terrible.

But her resolutions were forgotten when Susannah enfolded her in a long, warm hug on her return.

'Oh, Lewis, Lewis!' Fay cried aloud on her friend's shoulder. 'I can't have him, Susannah, I can't have him—and I love him more than ever, and his son, too!'

Susannah did not say a word; she just held Fay close as the tears flowed, the way Fay had comforted her when her own trouble had seemed too hard to bear.

CHAPTER NINE

FAY confided the basic facts of Lewis's situation to Susannah, knowing that her friend was absolutely trustworthy, but she could not convey the impressions that would stay in her heart and memory: the cosiness of the kitchen, the bustling north-country housewife, the three cats, the comfort of Lewis's bed and her dreams as she lay in it—and above all the innocent, trusting boy with Lewis's serious grey eyes, who had been so happy when she promised him that they would always be friends. . .and now she must betray those words and never visit Barfylde again.

The Trinidadian girl had never seen the usually optimistic Fay in such despair, and there seemed to be nothing she could say to comfort her.

'I'm sorry, love, this isn't much of a New Year for you,' apologised Fay, wiping her eyes on the last available tissue. 'Let's talk about *you* for a change.' She forced herself to smile. 'How was work today?'

Susannah hesitated for a moment. 'It was all right, but I'm going to ask Miss Clothier to put me on night duty. My maternity leave starts in two months' time, and I can do with the extra money.'

'Night duty? Oh, no, you won't get your proper sleep!' protested Fay. 'It will mean that you——'

'It will mean that I'll be tucked away out of sight,' said Susannah firmly. 'All of a sudden I've got bigger, and I'm so conscious of it, Fay. I don't mind the patients, bless them. They smile when they see me, and say, "Ah, *you* know all about it, Sister!" No, it's

141

everybody else—visitors, porters, technicians—the
place is full of staring eyes!'

'That's just your imagination,' remonstrated Fay. 'In
a maternity department of all places, what's so notice-
able about one more expectant mum?'

'A *lot*, when that mum is in uniform instead of a
nightie and dressing-gown,' sighed her friend. 'Like
yesterday morning—two ambulance men brought in a
new admission, and when I'd received her I heard them
joking to each other: "This is a baby factory right
enough! Even the nurses are on the production line!"
And I won't tell you what the other man said——'

She bit her lip, and Fay reacted at once, putting
aside her own unhappiness.

'Don't let it get to you, Susannah! It's because you're
feeling tired and less able to cope with rude remarks,
though I don't suppose they really meant any harm.
You know what insensitive brutes men can be.'

'It's all right, Fay, I'll be happier on nights,' said
Susannah. 'Come on, let's have a nice mug of hot
chocolate before we go to bed!'

Wearied by all the events of the past two days, Fay
thankfully crept under the duvet on her bed in the little
attic room, and slept until four o'clock, when she lay
staring out of the dormer window, praying for strength
and courage to face the days and weeks ahead.

She began to consider making a move away from
Beltonshaw. Her brother Roy was in the navy, and she
wondered what life would be like as a nursing sister in
the Women's Royal Naval Service. Or should she
transfer to the University Hospital and study for the
advanced diploma of midwifery, perhaps becoming a
tutor? Again, she could apply for a post as a community
midwife, and maybe take the health visitor's course in
a year or two. With a sigh, she eventually dismissed all

these possibilities because she could not work up enough enthusiasm for any of them; besides, there was Susannah, who would need her support for some time, before and after the baby's birth. I'd better not let Nicholas Lisle know about my unsettled state, she thought with a wry smile to herself, or he'll be after me again to join the staff of his birthing clinic. . .

Back on duty the next day, all the talk was about the double-page spread in the local paper about Joanna Leach's plans for her delivery in the birthing-room of Beltonshaw General Hospital. There were photographs of a smiling Joanna talking with Ann Clothier and Dr Lisle, and the one of Fay and Laurie taken on Christmas morning.

As Fay made her way back from lunch, she saw a used epidural trolley being wheeled out of Stage-One Room A. Her heart beat a little faster: was she about to confront Lewis Grant so soon after her secret visit to his home?

She was. Sister Pardoe had spread the paper on the office desk and was commenting about the Leach feature while Lewis completed an epidural record form.

'So, Sister Mitchell, you've got a famous face now!' teased the Scotswoman. 'Just look at this picture of you and Staff Nurse Moffatt! Mind you, I prefer it to the one of Miss Clothier and Dr Lisle grinning like Cheshire cats—don't *you*, Dr Grant?'

'Huh, we're certainly being treated to the full details of her plans,' he snorted. 'With husband Gordon cutting the umbilical cord and handing the baby straight to her for a breast-feed—I suppose the general public will revel in all this stuff.'

'Why, is it all written down there?' asked Fay in

pretended horror, though actually thankful for something to talk about, and for Sister Pardoe's presence.

'Oh, aye, Sister, and there's more to come!' went on the older midwife, her plain, good-humoured features alight with interest. 'It says here that the mother, father and baby are going to share a bath together after the delivery. Isn't that romantic?'

'Though perhaps a little messy,' ventured Fay with a shake of her head.

'And is Lisle going to strip off and join them in the water? Bit of a crush,' muttered Lewis, unsmilingly sarcastic.

'Why, now, Dr Grant, don't be naughty,' said Sister Pardoe reprovingly. 'We must be tolerant towards a pregnant lady who's never had a baby before, and doesn't know what she's in for.'

'I don't agree with you,' retorted Lewis. 'A primigravida of nearly forty should be properly informed and prepared to accept expert assistance when dear Mother Nature turns into an old bitch who won't co-operate with the birth-plan. This woman may well be in for a long and painful ordeal, and will probably need an epidural before she's halfway through it. *I'm* not prepared to fool around in the boudoir, so she'll end up being delivered up here in CDU, I'll stake my salary on it!'

His eyes flashed angrily and Fay decided to interpose.

'Don't let's anticipate trouble, Lewis,' she said gently. 'I've met Joanna, and she's an intelligent woman, quite easy to talk to. She knows that Mr Horsfield may intervene at any time, and she accepts that. She's also very fit. You never know, she *might* achieve all the aims of her birth-plan.'

'In which case *all* the antenatal patients will be

clamouring for the same treatment, and you midwives will have to cope with their disappointment and sense of failure when things *don't* go according to plan!' he snapped back.

'Fair enough, but let's try to keep a positive attitude,' answered Fay pleasantly. 'After all, seventy-five per cent of all births here are normal and supervised by midwives, without a white coat in sight.'

'And what about the twenty-five per cent who need a white coat in one hell of a hurry, Fay? Not just an obstetrician, but maybe a paediatrician as well, for God's sake!'

The two midwives looked up in surprise at such uncharacteristic language from Lewis, whose fury seemed almost out of control. He slammed his fist down on the newspaper as he got up and made for the door, where he turned round and faced them.

'Do you know what I'd like to say to that stupid journalist?' he asked savagely. 'All her talk of a mother's right to choose this or that mode of delivery— I'd point out to her that *babies* have rights as well, to be born by the safest method in any given set of circumstances. Only the poor little devils can't write out a bloody birth-plan!'

He stormed off down the corridor, and in her mind's eye Fay suddenly saw Tommy's eager little face with his father's eyes: the child who would never grow up, but who would go on haunting her, refusing to be banished from her thoughts. She ran to the door and called after the doctor.

'Lewis, wait! Please, I didn't mean——'

But he had gone, and Sister Pardoe laid a hand on Fay's shoulder.

'Shh, Sister, the poor man's no' himself these days. He has his reasons, no doubt, but we'll have no arguments on duty. Och, dearie me! He hasn't looked well for weeks, and he's getting worse.'

Fay checked herself from saying that she knew why Lewis had such apparently intolerant views on planned natural births. She composed her face and put away the newspaper before going to do a round of her antenatal patients.

However, the talk about Joanna had given her an idea: Tommy's pictures of the cats. . .surely Joanna would be an ideal person to approach for advice about a possible market? Yes! Fay decided to put the six sketches into a large envelope, backed with cardboard and accompanied by a personal letter to the journalist 'on behalf of a young friend'. She would then post them off to the Manchester offices of the national daily in which Joanna wrote her weekly column.

At four o'clock that afternoon there was an emergency admission: two grinning ambulance men brought in a stretcher trolley and deposited Jody Pockett on the examination couch in the admission-room.

'Here she is again, Sister! Must have got indigestion after the New Year!' one of them quipped.

Fay ignored the remark, and went to give the sulky, overweight girl a welcoming hug.

'Hi, Jody! Have your pains come on again? I'll put you on the monitor for half an hour, and make us both a nice cup of tea with two sugars in yours! Would you like a slice of toast as well?' she asked, and was rewarded by a grateful smile from poor bewildered Jody whose need for kindness and attention was just as great as Joanna's, and whose pregnancy was no less important to her.

As Fay brewed tea and made toast in the ward kitchen, she was suddenly aware of a white-coated figure standing at the door; looking up, she saw Lewis's pale face and shadowed eyes regarding her. She turned back to her task.

'Fay.' His voice was strained.

'Ah, Lewis, you've timed it just right for tea and toast,' she said with deliberate brightness. 'Poor Jody Pockett has come in again with yet another false alarm!'

'Fay, my dear, I'm sorry,' he said awkwardly.

'What for, Lewis?' Her tone was deceptively light as she put another slice of bread into the toaster and opened the refrigerator to get out some butter.

'For my boorish behaviour towards you and Sister Pardoe, of course. I had no right to express my views in that way, and I apologise.' He sounded so weary and dispirited that Fay longed to hold him in her arms and comfort him, though she had to hide her feelings behind a mask of professional concern.

'Are you well, Lewis?' she asked abruptly as she poured boiling water into the teapot to which she had added a third tea-bag.

'Well? What exactly do you mean, Fay?' he said in surprise.

'You're obviously under a lot of pressure, and that's what's making you irritable, isn't it?' She forced herself to look up at him as she spoke, as if he were a patient and she a friendly medical adviser. 'You seem to me to be thoroughly run-down and in need of a rest and a change,' she continued, putting the hot toast on three plates and spreading it generously with butter. It smelt delicious.

'It's strange that you should say that, Fay, because I've been thinking lately that I'm due for a change,' he replied, drumming his fingers on the Formica work surface. He seemed to be trying to bring himself to speak more frankly, and she waited with a pounding

heart as she arranged a tray for Jody and poured out
two steaming mugs of tea for themselves.

'I haven't treated you fairly, and I'm very sorry for
any wrong impression you've been given, Fay,' he said
at last. 'I had no right to—to show any interest in you
when my circumstances should have prevented me
from. . .' He hesitated, gripping his hands together so
tightly that the knuckles whitened. 'Actually, Fay, I've
decided to leave Beltonshaw,' he concluded.

She looked up quickly, and her heart ached at the
pain in his clouded grey eyes that seemed to reflect the
bleakness of the January day.

'Where will you go, Lewis?' Her hand shook as she
pushed a mug of tea and a plate of toast towards him,
and hastily swallowed a mouthful of tea from her own
mug.

'There's a vacancy in a general practice at Kirkby
Lonsdale, and I've applied for it,' he told her. 'It's not
too far from where I live, so I'll be able to keep a
better eye on my mother. She's getting on a bit now,
and could do with more support.'

Fay was unable to meet his eye or make any reply.
She literally held her breath as she waited for him to
continue. Did he suspect anything?

'The dear woman actually took in a complete
stranger to stay overnight on New Year's Eve,' he went
on. 'Some young girl who was wandering around in the
dark—could have been a thief or a nutcase, though it
seems she was harmless enough. Still, it's rather an
isolated area, and maybe now's the right time for me
to settle at home and keep an eye on things there.'

He paused and then added with a short laugh, 'So
I'll be leaving here at the end of February, and I think
you'll be well rid of me, Fay.'

Fay stood very still.

'I shall miss you, of course, Lewis, but perhaps you're doing the best thing in the circumstances. I'd been thinking about a move myself, though for the time being there's Susannah to——'

She stopped speaking and looked out of the window, choking back tears; then she resolutely picked up Jody's tray.

'I'm sorry, Lewis, but I can't drink tea and eat toast and cry all at the same time. Excuse me, please, I must go to Jody!'

She briefly brushed past him as she left the kitchen, and he stood staring at her back as she walked up the corridor. For a moment he covered his face with his hand, then straightened up and went in the other direction.

''Ave you got a cold, Sister Mitchell?' asked Jody, her eyes brightening at the sight of the tray.

'No, Jody, it's just that I've been drinking scalding-hot tea!' answered Fay with the friendly smile that her patients always saw.

When Fay went off duty at nine that evening, she ran into Matthew Okoje on her way out of the hospital gates.

'Ah, the very man I want to see!' she said eagerly.

'May I wish you a happy New Year, Fay?' he asked significantly.

'Of course, and the same to you. Look, Matthew, can we talk?'

'Certainly, I'm free this evening,' he replied. 'Would you like to go to the Outsiders for a drink and a snack, maybe?'

'Yes—er—no, Matthew. Come home with me for some supper,' she said with sudden decision. 'We can talk as we walk.'

'But what about Su—your friend Sister Starr?' he asked anxiously, though his eyes expressed a longing to see the woman he loved.

'*What* about Susannah? We're all friends, aren't we?' smiled Fay, linking her arm through his as they set off. 'Listen, Matthew, I want to remind you that what we said on Christmas Day was absolutely confidential— about Lewis, I mean.'

'But you know I would never tell anybody!' he protested.

'Lewis must never know that I went to his house and pryed into his private life,' she insisted. 'I changed my name, so he won't find out from Mollie—I mean his mother. And I must just pretend that I don't know about the existence of Tommy—oh, Matthew! I can't bear to think about it——'

Her voice broke, and the Ugandan doctor tightened his hold on her arm, his honest face full of sympathy and regret.

'I should never have given you his address, Fay! It was wrong of me when I knew that he didn't want you to know. Please forgive me!'

'It's all right, don't blame yourself,' she told him. 'I'd have found out by one means or another, and at least I now know why Lewis keeps me at a distance. And now he's leaving Beltonshaw. . .it's for the best, I suppose. As long as he never finds out that I went to Barfylde!'

'He will never find out from me, Fay,' Matthew assured her solemnly, placing his hand over hers for a moment. 'I am sorry that you do not feel you can go further. I had a hope you would take to Tommy——'

'Please, Matthew, don't say any more!' she begged. 'I've got to forget that I ever set eyes on him, and it's *agony*, so please don't mention the subject again, ever!'

Matthew was startled by the vehemence of her words and tone, and they walked the rest of the way in silence. When they arrived at number thirty-seven Grange Road, Fay almost had to push him inside the front door.

'Hi, Abigail! Here's nice Dr Okoje come to see us!' she called, running up the stairs while Abigail and Matthew greeted each other.

'Coo-ee, Susannah! Er—Matthew Okoje's come for a bite of supper with us,' she said quickly as Susannah got up from her chair with a look of dismay.

'Now don't be *silly*, love, stay where you are while I make a cheese omelette for the three of us,' she told her friend firmly. 'I had to speak to him about— Lewis—and it was only courtesy to ask him in for a snack on a night like this. Ah, there you are, Matthew—enter our humble abode and talk to Susannah while I put the kettle on!'

The embarrassment of the Trinidadian girl gradually gave way to shy smiles in response to Matthew's impeccable good manners and deferential approach to her. She was wearing a loosely flowing caftan in various shades of blue which looked very becoming on her Junoesque figure. Fay heard their hesitant exchange of New Year greetings and comments about the cold weather as she poured boiling water into three mugs of instant coffee.

Susannah will reproach me for this later, but I'm doing Matthew a favour, she thought, and now it's up to him to follow the lead I've given him!

CHAPTER TEN

JANUARY slowly crept by in a succession of wet days
and lowering skies that made the wards so dark that
the lights needed to be on almost all day. Susannah
went on night duty, and number thirty-seven Grange
Road was plunged into silence while she slept; Abigail
would allow no radio, vacuum cleaner or washing
machine to be used while Susannah was in bed, and
Fay was grateful for the motherly fussing which
relieved her of responsibility for her friend, who had
lately become more relaxed and seemed much happier.
February came in bringing drier, colder weather.

When Sister Pardoe had to go off duty with influenza, Fay was asked to work extra hours to cover for
staff shortage; she was quite willing to do so, as work
was her only comfort during these dark days, and
helped to keep her from brooding over Lewis and what
she saw as the tragedy of his life. Nevertheless, the
extended shifts of duty and the cancelled days off
began to take their toll, and the strain showed in her
pale features and the blue-grey smudges beneath her
eyes. Little did she realise how much these signs
troubled Lewis Grant, for he kept his distance and hid
his concern behind a stern detachment that only the
patients were able to penetrate.

Like poor Jody Pockett, who after so many false
alarms actually went a week overdue, and Mr Horsfield
decided upon an induction of labour. Jody was terrified
at the very thought, and when Lewis happened to come
into the antenatal ward just after Mr Horsfield's round

he found Jody sobbing out her fears to Fay, who had not really got time to sit and talk in the middle of a busy morning. Lewis at once sat down on Jody's bed, and in a friendly, gently teasing manner he calmed and reassured the frightened girl who was all too ready to listen to the horror stories and 'old wives' tales' of her mother. As he chatted with her and asked what names she had planned to call the baby, the ward clerk appeared and beckoned Fay to the office to take a personal telephone call. Immediately concerned for Susannah, Fay picked up the receiver and gave her name.

'My dear Fay! Are you busy? Joanna Leach—remember?'

'Oh! Good morning—er—Joanna. How are you keeping?' asked Fay in surprise.

'Fine! Apart from getting a bit tired by the end of the day, pregnancy is marvellous! I can't understand why any woman shouldn't enjoy every moment of it! Look, Fay, I'm calling about those pictures you sent me—those incredible sketches of cats by that young friend of yours, you know?'

'Oh, *yes!*' exclaimed Fay, her heart suddenly thumping.

'The art department here were very impressed, and a contact of mine took them to Thorpe's—you know, the greetings card people—and, my dear, they're *raving* over them, honestly! They want to meet the artist and see more of his work, so shall I put them in touch with you?'

'Oh. . . Joanna. . .' Fay was unable to marshal her thoughts together, and felt that she needed time to think of a plan that would not involve herself.

'Are you still there, Fay?' asked Joanna as Fay gasped and searched for words.

'Yes, I—it's wonderful news, and I—I shall have to let my friend know,' she managed to reply.

'Look, I'll put you in touch with Thorpe's, and you can sort it out with them,' suggested Joanna. She gave Fay a London telephone number, and told her to mention Joanna's name. 'They'll be delighted to hear from you, and may I add my own congratulations to your talented young friend?' concluded the columnist in her charming way.

'Thank you very much, Joanna, you're most kind,' mumbled Fay, replacing the receiver just as Lewis entered the office.

'Oh, that poor girl!' he sighed, shaking his head sadly. 'What chance has she ever had, with a stupid mother and that lout of a boyfriend who doesn't care tuppence for her? God help her and the baby!'

'Thanks for your help with her, Lewis,' said Fay a little breathlessly. 'I expect she'll need an epidural once her contractions really start.'

'Which won't be too easy, with all that surplus fat she's carrying,' he commented wryly. 'Haven't you spoken to her about dieting?'

'*You* try!' retorted Fay. 'She's had consultations with the dietician, loads of advice and leaflets, and the kitchen sends up a very carefully planned diet for reducing during pregnancy. The trouble is, her mother brings in an endless supply of sweets and biscuits because she says we're starving her daughter!'

As it turned out, there was no induction after all. At teatime Jody frantically rang the call-bell to say that she was getting pains in her tummy and back, and when Fay went to examine her a sudden gush of water indicated that the membranes had ruptured, and the cervix was already halfway dilated. Jody was hastily transferred to the delivery unit, and before the visitors arrived at seven she was proudly sitting up with her baby son in her plump arms. She announced that he was to be called Lewis, and her mother always maintained that Jody had been frightened into labour by the threat of 'one of them injunctions'.

When Fay wearily returned to number thirty-seven, she found a bulky envelope from her father; it contained a letter from him and another letter and a picture postcard, both addressed to Miss Faith Marsden at her father's Nethersedge address.

'I don't know what this is all about, *Miss Marsden*,' her father had written. 'You obviously have a reason for concealing your surname and location from somebody, but you've certainly made a hit with the young man who wrote the postcard.'

Fay stared at the card, which showed a farmyard scene; then she read the few lines Tommy Grant had written on the back:

Dear Faith, I miss you, and so does Mrs Black, Podger and Tinker. We want to see you again, so please come *soon*. I love you, Faith. From Tommy X X X.

Fay closed her eyes, feeling that she could not possibly ignore such a plea; yet how could she answer it? With trembling fingers she opened the other letter which she guessed was from Mollie Grant. It was short but to the point.

Dear Faith,
I hope you are keeping well. I am asking you to come and visit Tommy, who has been poorly with a bad cold and never stops asking for you. I am sending enough money to pay your fare, and train and bus

timetables. Please telephone to let me know when to expect you. I need to see you and talk to you.

Yours truly,
Mollie Grant.

A cheque for fifty pounds was neatly folded between the timetables which dealt with services throughout the north-west.

Fay knew that she had to respond to this summons, even if it meant that she might have to take Mollie into her confidence. Knowing that Lewis's duties allowed him every alternate weekend free, she could be reasonably sure of not coinciding with him if she visited Barfylde on her next day off, a Wednesday. She dialled the number of Pear Tree Cottage, and Mrs Grant answered.

'I thought you were taking no heed to my letter, Faith, it were last week that I wrote,' she said bluntly as soon as she heard Fay's voice.

'I'm very sorry, Mollie, but your letter was delayed. How's Tommy now?' asked Fay.

'Still coughing, and not much appetite, but a sight o' you would do him good. You've got money for t' fare, so can you take time to come?'

'Yes, Mollie, I'll come on Wednesday. The train will bring me to within about six miles of Barfylde, and I'll get a taxi from there. I shan't be able to stay overnight, but I'll spend the afternoon with you and Tommy. Give him my love, and——'

'Faith! Faith! Please come to see me!' came an eager, slightly hoarse voice on the line, and Fay could only reply, 'Yes, darling Tommy, I'm coming.' She had to make a great effort to keep her voice steady.

'Promise?'

'I promise, Tommy, I promise.'

* * *

Fay paid the taxi-driver at the bottom of Ively Lane, and walked up the unpaved track and over the tree-crowned summit that brought her in sight of Pear Tree Cottage. It was midday, and the sky had cleared to give a burst of winter sunshine; she remembered the occasion over a month ago when she had approached this house in fear of what she would find—and now she had been summoned back to it.

As soon as Tommy saw her from the window where he was watching, he rushed out of the house to meet her. Fay too instinctively broke into a run, and as they hugged each other in the lane she experienced again a conviction that here was her destiny, no matter what the circumstances. Hand in hand she and the boy walked to join his grandmother, who stood at the gate regarding them with a strange expression; her gaunt features softened, and Fay thought that her bony figure showed the effects of years of hard work as an unsupported widow, and then having to care for Lewis's child.

'You're right welcome, lass, and dinner's nearly ready for t' table. Don't let our Tommy take up all your time, but step into t' kitchen and warm yourself,' she said in her down-to-earth manner. Her penetrating grey eyes made Fay feel rather uncomfortable, and as the three of them ate roast pork and apple sauce at the kitchen table, listening to Tommy's chatter about his daddy's last visit to them, Fay knew that she had to undeceive Molly Grant without delay, as well as returning the cheque.

As soon as dinner was cleared away and tea brewed, Fay told Tommy to draw her a special picture of Mrs Black asleep on the bench seat, and asked Mollie if they could take the tea-tray into another room. The older woman nodded without surprise, and led the way into a parlour where a wood fire crackled in the hearth.

'I lit it before dinner to warm t' room for us,' said Mollie. 'Now sit here beside me, lass, and tell me what you have to say.'

Fay's hands trembled, and she put down her cup and saucer.

'There's no need to fear t' truth, Faith, and happen I know some of it already,' prompted Mollie quietly. Fay looked straight into the eyes of Lewis's mother, and found the courage to speak.

She began simply, 'I came here under false pretences, Mollie, so I must ask you to forgive me. I've known your son Dr Grant for some time, and I wanted to find out why he—why he kept himself apart from me when it was obvious to us both that he and I——' She broke off, unable to find the right words, and then continued, 'I just had to know what it was that he wouldn't tell me, you see!'

Mollie sighed and nodded. 'I know, lass. In fact I began to suspect summat o' that sort when you came here first. Then Lewis brought *this* home, and I knew for certain.'

She reached under a cushion on the settee where they sat, and produced a copy of the paper. There in front of Fay was the Joanna Leach feature, with the photograph of herself and Laurie Moffatt on Christmas morning.

Sister Fay Mitchell, a midwife at Beltonshaw General Hospital, led Joanna on a tour of the antenatal ward.

Fay blushed crimson, and gasped, 'Oh, *no*! Did you tell Lewis that you recognised me?'

'Nay, lass, I kept my own counsel when he showed

me the picture of his special midwife,' smiled Mollie reassuringly, 'and I managed to keep it out of our Tommy's way. But I wasn't sorry, Faith, and because I'd met you and seen you with Tommy I thought to myself, She's the right woman for my son. I kept quiet, but I want you to have him, Faith. I want him to marry you.'

'But I can't, I *can't*!' cried Fay wildly. 'Lewis already has a wife, even though she has deserted him—he's not free to marry anybody while she's living! Oh, Mollie, I could soon convince Lewis that I love Tommy and would be so happy to take care of him, but it's the problem of Tommy's mother that just can't be overcome!'

Covering her face with her hands, she burst into tears.

Lewis Grant's mother sat looking at her in stunned silence for a few moments, and then she began to speak, slowly and with reluctance, her face and voice full of regret.

'So *that's* what you thought, you poor little lass, just because I'm such a stupid old woman and didn't tell you the truth. You'll have to forgive me, Faith.'

Faith looked up in bewilderment. 'Forgive *you*, Mollie?'

'Aye, for being ashamed of my son's past, and not being honest wi' you about Tommy's mother.'

Fay wiped her eyes and braced herself for whatever else she had to hear. 'Go on, Mollie.'

'Lewis has never been married. She were never his wife.'

Fay's dark eyes widened. '*What*? For heaven's sake, Mollie, what do you mean?'

'He were only twenty-three and in medical school,' muttered Mollie quickly, as if the words were being forced out. 'She were another student, an actress o' sorts, and he were right daft about her and couldn't see sense. When she was expecting his child, he wanted to marry her, but she didn't want to be tied down, she said. They lived in a little flat, and she set her mind on having t' baby there instead of in t' hospital. It were a nightmare, wi' her screaming t' place down, and t' baby wrong way round—she wouldn't heed Lewis, though later she blamed him for everything when she upped and left. He's never forgiven himself, though he were only a medical student at the time, and God knows he's paid for his mistake, Faith, over and over again. You're right, he does love you, but he says he can't burden you with poor Tommy. A liability, he calls him——'

'Oh, how *could* he?' asked Fay indignantly. 'My Tommy!'

'That's what I thought you'd say,' agreed Mollie with a certain pride in her own judgement. 'You're the right one for them *both*, and I want to see you all happy together before I get too old to cope.'

'Shh, Mollie, don't upset yourself,' said Fay, taking the woman's restless hands in both of her own. 'I need time to take all of this in, but what you've just told me changes everything. Don't say anything to Lewis about me, will you? He's suffered so much, and I'll have to let him know in my own way. Leave it to me, Mollie, and don't worry.'

'Just as you wish, Faith—only answer me one question. Do you really want to marry my son?'

Fay smiled through her tears of relief and joy. 'Do I? I'll say I do! Why else did I risk coming all this way on New Year's Eve, not knowing what I was going to find? You might have turned out to be an old witch or something!' She chuckled. 'We're going to be friends, you and I, Mother.'

Their impulsive embrace was interrupted by Tommy who ran in with his picture of Mrs Black.

'It's *very* good, Tommy!' exclaimed Fay in renewed admiration as she examined the vividly conveyed impression of lithe limbs in repose. 'And do you know something? Your pictures are going to be printed on birthday cards and calendars, and you'll be paid money for them—yes, really! That's something else I've got to tell you, Mollie—we've got a professional artist in the family!'

When Fay returned that night to number thirty-seven, she felt that she did not yet want to confide in Susannah. She had to see Lewis first, and bring all misunderstandings to an end before telling even her closest friend about her new hopes of happiness. Yet how could she conceal the truth from dear Susannah who had comforted her when she had thought that Lewis was lost to her forever? She knew that Susannah was not on duty, and would be waiting for her in their flat.

The problem was solved in a way that Fay could hardly have imagined. Susannah had other matters on her mind as she stood up and greeted Fay with a loving hug; her face was radiant as she then brought forward Matthew Okoje who was waiting with her for Fay's return.

'We wanted you to be the first to know, because you've been such a good friend to us both. Matthew has asked me to marry him!' announced the Trinidadian girl in joyful wonder as Fay stared at each of them in turn, her eyes alight with amazement and delight.

'Don't pretend to be surprised, Fay—you and
Matthew have been plotting away behind my back, so
he tells me!' her friend accused her amid the laughter,
kisses and congratulations that ensued.

'When's the wedding?' asked Fay when she could
pause for breath.

'Just as soon as we can get a licence!' affirmed
Matthew with a determined look in his fiancée's
direction.

'But it will be a very quiet ceremony,' insisted
Susannah, 'just ourselves and my pastor at the
Pentecostal Church.'

'But you'll need to have two witnesses present,' Fay
pointed out.

'Yes, and the only two people we can possibly ask
are our best and dearest friends,' smiled Susannah
shyly. 'Matthew wants Lewis Grant there with him,
and I want you. Do you mind, Fay?'

The happy couple were assured that Fay would not
mind at all.

There was a keen frost that night, and Fay had to walk
carefully the next morning; at half-past seven it was
still too dark to see the icy patches on the pavement.
The cold air nipped her nose as her breath rose in
visible clouds, yet inwardly she glowed with the warmth
of her happiness at the thought of seeing Lewis again.
How soon would that meeting be, and how would she
find the right words to tell him that she knew everything
now? When would she have the opportunity to speak
to him alone and at leisure? Would it be today? Father
Naylor's words came back to her mind: 'May you be
guided in the right direction, Faith!' And so she had
been, through all the obstacles of misunderstanding
and heartbreak. She smiled to herself, and clasped her

gloved hands in anticipation: nothing now stood in the way of their love!

As soon as she reported on duty, she found the maternity department buzzing with the news that Joanna Leach had been admitted to the birthing-room late the previous evening, a full two weeks before her official delivery date.

'Dr Lisle's been up all night with her,' said chatty Night Sister Hicks. 'When I heard that Miss Clothier had gone to bed at one o'clock, I guessed that Joanna couldn't be that far on in labour. Mr Horsfield's coming in to see her this morning, and I wouldn't be surprised if he transfers her up here.'

'Poor Joanna!' smiled Fay. 'She's so set her heart on a completely natural childbirth, hasn't she?'

'Yes, and after all she's written about it, it will be a big let-down if she doesn't achieve one,' shrugged Sister Hicks, buttoning up her navy gabardine prior to cycling home to her welcoming bed.

The morning hours went by, and Fay was kept busy with her antenatal patients as well as assisting in the delivery unit because of Sister Pardoe's absence. After supervising a straightforward normal delivery with a student midwife just before two, she left the ward in the charge of Staff Nurse Moffatt while she went for a curtailed afternoon off.

Hurrying out of the hospital gates, she suddenly found herself face to face with Lewis Grant coming in.

'Oh, hello! How are you, Lewis?' she asked shyly, hoping for a chance to talk, and seeing his mother's face in his pale, gaunt features.

'My dear girl, you look worn out!' he said sternly. 'Are you off now for the rest of the day?'

'No, I'm doing a split shift,' she replied, furious with herself for blushing crimson under his scrutiny.

'What, another one? Try to get some rest this afternoon,' he advised, frowning as he continued on his way.

She nodded and walked off briskly down the road, wondering if he had yet been told the news about Matthew and Susannah. She felt sure that he would be pleased at the way things had turned out for those two, but this did not seem a good time to ask.

She did not know that Lewis had stopped and was staring at her retreating back as he recollected words that his mother had spoken on his last visit home.

'A tidy little body with a dark, curly head and a friendly manner o' speaking: it were the way she took to our Tommy and he to her.'

Lewis wondered why he should suddenly think about that mysterious girl hiker as his mother's words continued to run through his head.

'Said she came from Kendal way, a place called Nethersedge—and she'd got friends at Beltonshaw.'

Hadn't Fay said that her father had moved to Westmorland on his re-marriage?

'Our Tommy's done nowt but ask to see Faith again, and she were that taken with his pictures o' the cats!'

Faith? But the girl had been barely twenty, and worked in a day nursery or something—whereas Fay would be twenty-six this year, though everybody said she looked young for her age. . .

Lewis gave himself a shake and strode towards the hospital's accident and emergency entrance. Somehow he would have to learn to banish Fay Mitchell from his thoughts, and the sooner he left Beltonshaw the better, he told himself severely.

When Fay returned to duty at five, Laurie Moffatt looked ruffled.

'Ooh, you've missed a right hullabaloo this afternoon!' she said. 'Mr Horsfield ordered Joanna Leach to be transferred up to CDU for continuous foetal monitoring, and Miss Clothier's furious!'

'Really? At least I'll be able to look in on Joanna, then,' said Fay. 'Is she progressing in labour?'

'I haven't a clue,' replied the big blonde girl. 'Dr Lisle and Miss Clothier are with her in Delivery-Room Two, and nobody else is allowed in there.'

'Indeed? Well, as I've been asked to take charge of the delivery unit this evening, I shall expect to have access to every patient being cared for in it,' asserted Fay with quiet determination. 'Is there anybody else in labour?'

'No. One lady just delivered, and Dr Gillis is putting in some stitches—then she can be transferred to Postnatal.'

'Good. Thank you, Laurie. Enjoy your evening off!' said Fay, bracing herself for action.

As Laurie left the office, Nicholas Lisle entered, looking tired and annoyed. He fervently wished that he had followed Miss Clothier's example and got some sleep the previous night; Joanna's labour was proving to be slow and tedious.

'Ah, Fay, the very girl we need,' he said wearily. 'Joanna's been asking for you all day. Could you come and see her?'

'Certainly, Dr Lisle,' replied Fay pleasantly, adding with a sly little sideways glance, 'It's ideal for the mothers, isn't it, to have continuity of care throughout labour from one person? Joanna must be so thankful for you and Miss Clothier!'

His only reply was a yawn as he followed Fay to Delivery-Room Two where Joanna was sitting up on the specially constructed bed, supported by her husband and Ann Clothier. She was gritting her teeth as another contraction seized her uterine muscles.

'Oh, Fay, I'm so glad to see you!' she gasped, her large violet eyes clouded with pain and fatigue. 'I had no idea that this was going to go on for so *long*. Could I ask your opinion about——?'

'You're doing *marvellously*, Joanna,' gushed Miss Clothier, giving Fay a condescending nod. 'This is how a mother should participate in the birthing process! She's a perfect example of our technique, isn't she, Nicholas?'

The self-consciously girlish laugh which the senior midwife reserved for Lisle and the glance she threw in his direction could only be described as flirtatious, though his red-rimmed eyes did not respond to her enthusiasm.

'Hi, Joanna, how's it going?' enquired Fay quietly, taking hold of the patient's hand.

'I'm glad you're here, Fay, because I want to ask your opinion about epidural anaesthetics,' said Joanna breathlessly.

Miss Clothier hastily intervened.

'Joanna, dear, just persevere with your relaxation and deep breathing exercises, and there shouldn't be any need for an epidural and all the inconveniences that go with it,' she almost pleaded. 'Remember your birth-plan!'

'I didn't know about labour pains when I wrote *that*!' muttered Joanna as she clutched at her tense abdomen with a suppressed groan. 'How many more of these contractions have I got to live through?'

Gordon Swayne, irritable with sleeplessness and anxiety, turned to Lisle and snapped, 'For heaven's sake, it's been eighteen hours! If my wife wants an epidural, let her have one!'

'I mustn't let everybody down, Fay—my readers must never be disillusioned with me,' begged Joanna. 'Just get me an epidural, Fay, *please*!'

Fay caught Lisle's eye briefly and noted his nod of agreement. She avoided looking at Ann Clothier, but winked at Joanna.

'I'll get the anaesthetist right away, love.'

Lewis Grant wasted no words when he entered the delivery-room. Fay had prepared the epidural trolley while Miss Clothier had assisted Lisle to put up an intravenous drip in readiness. Ignoring them all, Lewis went straight to Joanna.

'Good evening, Mrs Swayne. I'm Dr Lewis Grant, anaesthetic registrar,' he told her reassuringly. 'Do you understand how an epidural works, and has anybody told you about possible side-effects?'

'Fay Mitchell sent for you, and that's good enough for me, Dr Grant,' answered Joanna, visibly relaxing as she sensed his air of authority. Gordon sighed with relief as Lewis speedily set about relieving the agony of prolonged labour in a primigravida of nearly forty. Lisle slipped away quietly, hoping to take a quick nap, and Miss Clothier looked daggers at Fay.

'My God, what a difference! I can *cope* with the contractions now!' cried Joanna in amazed delight. 'Gordon, this doctor's a miracle-worker!'

'Not at all, Mrs Swayne, thank modern technology,' said Lewis. 'The pains will come back in an hour or two, but Miss Clothier or Sister Mitchell will be able to give you a top-up of the local anaesthetic.'

His features softened, and for the first time he looked straight at Fay. Her dark eyes were brimming over with love and her lips curved in a tender smile as she held his gaze; he caught his breath momentarily.

'Right!' snapped Miss Clothier, bustling to take

Joanna's blood-pressure. 'Now we can let Dr Grant go back to his other patients, and I'm sure that Sister has lots of work to do, too!'

She was almost shooing them out of the room when Joanna, freed from pain and able to give her mind to other matters, called out to Fay.

'What happened about those pictures, Fay? You know, those fantastic sketches of cats you sent me? Did your young friend get in touch with Thorpe's?'

Fay froze. Lewis spun round abruptly, and stared first at Joanna and then at Fay, who turned away, desperately hoping that Miss Clothier would dismiss them both quickly.

But Lewis returned to the bedside.

'Excuse me, Mrs Swayne, did you say pictures of *cats*?' he asked, speaking with an effort. 'May I ask what sort of pictures they were?'

'Fay will tell you!' replied Joanna brightly. 'She's got a clever young friend—a boy who does marvellous original studies of——'

Miss Clothier interrupted sharply.

'Joanna, dear, *do* try to rest now. And please leave us *at once*, Sister Mitchell!'

Fay was only too glad to obey, and rushed out into the annexe of the delivery unit, intending to return to the office; but a firm detaining hand caught her by the shoulder, turning her round and forcing her to look up into Lewis's burning eyes. Never had she seen him look so alive, so animated as realisation dawned in their grey depths—and as she looked up helplessly at him the full knowledge blazed between them. She felt the steel grip of his hands on her shoulders, and her slender body trembled before this man whose life had become so inextricably linked with her own.

And then he spoke.

'It was you. Of course! Oh, my little Fay, it had to be you, didn't it? And I think I've known all along, ever since I telephoned home on New Year's Day— you must have been there! Yes, of course. . .'

His words trailed off as he saw the joy in her answering look; her brilliant eyes were shining with tears that she could not restrain.

'Let's step in here,' she whispered, pulling him into the theatre changing-room, a little cubby-hole where they could bolt the door and have a few moments of privacy.

'I was waiting for the right moment to tell you, Lewis, but now Joanna has said it for me,' she said breathlessly. 'I didn't intend it to be like this! I went to Barfylde again yesterday on my day off, and your mother and I talked. She knows, Lewis—and I know everything, too. You'll have to forgive me. *She* has.'

He stared in disbelief.

'Yesterday? My mother *knows*?'

'Yes.'

'But, Fay, *why* did you go there?'

'To find out what you wouldn't tell me, Lewis—and now I know.'

'But—why did you go back again yesterday?'

She answered him boldly, her eyes meeting his. 'Because Tommy needed me, Lewis—*he's* the reason I went back again. Tommy loves me, Lewis, your mother will tell you that. And I love him, and I've promised that we'll always be friends. Oh, can't you understand?'

At the mention of his son's name his brow had darkened, and a shadow crossed his face, that shadow that she had seen so many times before; it had fallen between them on every occasion that they had drawn close.

'You don't realise, Fay, you can't understand what

it's like to have the lifelong responsibility for a retarded child,' he said gravely, as if a heavy weight had descended upon him. 'My son won't always look like a boy. He'll get older and bigger and more difficult to deal with. He's someone I'm responsible for, and can't ask any woman to share. Certainly not *you*.'

She drew back from him in sudden indignation.

'Why *not* me?' she demanded. 'Why do you want to keep us apart, Tommy and me? We *love* each other, Lewis, and I'd love him even if he weren't your son! I want to share Tommy with you, can't you see? Your mother understands, so why can't you?'

He turned away with a gesture of despair.

'You mustn't let youself be influenced by my mother, Fay. She doesn't see him as I do. To her he's a very special child.'

'Of course he's a very special child!' Fay almost shouted. 'How do *you* see him, then, your son who worships you, your own flesh and blood?'

'Naturally I'm deeply attached to him as his father,' protested Lewis, struggling with conflicting emotions, 'but you surely must also realise what a liability he is— my illegitimate, brain-damaged son! He'll always be *there*, can't you see? A life-sentence!'

All of a sudden Fay exploded with a fierce anger that took both of them by surprise.

'How *dare* you? How *could* you say such a thing about my Tommy?' she stormed. 'Don't you ever call him that again to me, do you hear? My God! Don't you realise that he is an artist with a unique talent that neither you nor I have got? Have you no appreciation of his sweet nature, his innocence, his capacity for loving? Oh, *damn* you, Lewis Grant, you don't deserve to have such a son!'

Lewis backed away from her in genuine alarm. He

felt as if he was facing a tigress whose cub he had injured in some way, and yet at the same time he knew that he had never loved her more than now. Was she going to strike him? he wondered for a moment. If so, he felt that he deserved it.

But Fay burst into tears and dashed out of the changing-room, wrenching herself free of his detaining arm. She ran out of the annexe and down the corridor to the office.

'Fay! Fay, please, *wait!*' he called after her, but she kept going until she reached the office where Dr Rose Gillis and a student midwife looked up in some embarrassment, having heard their upraised voices.

'I say, Fay, love, are you all right? Do you need a cup of tea?' asked Rose with professional calm.

'No—I mean yes—I'm sorry,' muttered Fay, brushing away the tears with the back of her hand. The student midwife silently handed her a box of tissues and tactfully left the office.

Rose got up and put a friendly arm around Fay's shaking shoulders.

'I don't know what all *that* was about, but I'll tell you what I do know,' she said. 'Lewis Grant is crazy about you. And as he's a very good man, I just hope that you two can sort things out—OK?'

'Oh, Rose!' Just for a moment Fay buried her face against the friendly shoulder before a discreet cough at the door made them both look up to see Mr Horsfield peering over the top of his gold-rimmed spectacles.

'Are you all right, Sister, dear?' he enquired kindly.

'Yes, sir, perfectly,' answered Fay, instantly composing herself.

'Good. I've come to take another look at Joanna. If she hasn't made any further progress, I may decide to cut a long story short and do a Caesarean section. I've

just seen Grant and told him that it can be done under
his epidural. Is Lisle around?'

'I believe so, sir.'

Fay immediately straightened her white cap and
accompanied the consultant to Delivery-Room Two.

As it turned out, Joanna Leach was able to achieve the
main points of her birth-plan. After the epidural had
been commenced her tension and fear subsided, and
labour progressed well from then on. Mr Horsfield was
satisfied as to the condition of mother and baby, and
he agreed to let her continue in labour under his own
close surveillance, which Miss Clothier had to accept
with as good a grace as she could assume.

At a quarter to eight the cervix was fully dilated:
stage two of labour had commenced, and Joanna was
encouraged to push down hard with each contraction.
Dr Lisle was summoned from the residency where he
had fallen asleep, and Mr Horsfield gave in to Joanna's
request to have Fay beside her during the final strong,
expulsive contractions, much to Ann Clothier's inward
fury.

So when Lewis Grant put his head round the door to
see how things were going he saw Joanna gripping her
husband's hand on one side and Fay's on the other,
while Ann Clothier and Nicholas Lisle chorused in
unison,

'Another push, Joanna! Give us another push, go
on, harder—harder—harder!'

Their authority was much diminished by Mr
Horsfield's watchful presence, and Fay was extremely
thankful that the consultant was there, disarming Miss
Clothier's resentment of her, enabling her to whisper
comforting words to Joanna, who was by now very
tired. Gordon Swayne looked ready to drop after his

twenty-four-hour vigil, but braced himself to help his wife in her desperate effort to give birth to their long-awaited child.

Lewis took in this scene at a glance, and was about to withdraw his head when Joanna caught sight of him.

'Dr Grant! Don't go away, please!' she called out.

'Come in, Grant,' nodded Mr Horsfield. 'Joanna's been telling us all about the joys of epidural anaesthesia. Pity you weren't called to give it earlier. Never mind, we're nearly home now.'

Lewis entered noiselessly and stood with his back against the door. Without turning round to look at him, Fay was conscious of the warmth of his presence, that sense of safety she always felt when he was around. She flushed deeply at the thought of how she had spoken to him only a couple of hours ago, and yet deep down in her heart she felt that he would not hold it against her: she had made an important declaration when she had defended her strong attachment to Tommy.

Joanna's frenzied twisting of her hand recalled her to the duties of the moment. The baby's head had failed to advance during the last contraction, and Joanna was beginning to panic as the pain returned.

'I can't do it! I can't do it! I *can't*, I tell you!' wailed the exhausted woman as Miss Clothier begged her to push harder. A flicker of deceleration showed on the foetal heart monitor.

'Episiotomy, Lisle.' Mr Horsfield's words were a command, and Nicholas at once set about performing the clean incision of the perineum that widened the outlet sufficiently to let the baby's head emerge. Fay whispered explanations to Joanna and Gordon, and within two minutes the great moment arrived.

Ann Clothier, red-faced and perspiring, announced, 'You've got a little girl, Joanna!'

Gordon suppressed a sob of relief, and kissed his wife's forehead.

Fay smiled and said, 'I knew you could do it!'

Mr Horsfield beamed. 'Well done!'

Nicholas Lisle, his eyes red-rimmed with sleeplessness, muttered, 'Thank God that's over at last!'

Lewis Grant unobtrusively withdrew. Out in the corridor he met Roger the photographer, who had been hanging around all day; he sighed with relief when Lewis gave him the thumbs-up sign, and adjusted his camera for the first mother-and-baby pictures.

The drama was not quite over, however. After the expulsion of the placenta, Joanna's tired muscles failed to tighten sufficiently to stop the flow of blood, and at least half a litre was immediately lost. Mr Horsfield stepped forward and expertly squeezed Joanna's tummy to encourage the empty uterus to contract, at the same time ordering Lisle to add ten units of syntocinon to the drip. The haemorrhage was brought under control, and Fay breathed a silent prayer of thanks that the patient was in the consultant delivery unit.

It had been another very long day, and Fay was late giving the report to Night Sister Hicks, who had come on duty eager to hear the news of Joanna. When the handing over was completed and the drugs checked, Fay put on her navy gabardine and made her way down the stairs to the ground-floor exit.

To her amazement she found Ann Clothier standing waiting for her near to the door.

'Just a minute, I want a word with you!' the senior midwife barked.

'Who—me?' asked Fay in bewilderment.

'Yes, *you*, Sister Mitchell!' cried Ann, trembling all over. 'This time you've gone too far, and I'm not standing for it any longer—pushing yourself forward, fawning over Horsfield and my own special patient! You don't fool *me*, even if you fool them! I can see through your game, and you won't get away with it, he won't give you the clinic job!'

'What on earth are you talking about, Miss Clothier?' asked Fay, her hand on the end of the stair-rail. 'Please try to get a grip on yourself, or at least wait until we can talk somewhere more private than this.'

'Don't you *dare* to patronise me!' returned Ann, her voice shrill with anger and fatigue. 'You're jealous of me, aren't you, Mitchell? You want that post in the Lisle Birthing Clinic, and you don't like it because he's giving it to me. Oh, I know, I know—you thought you'd bewitched Nicholas, didn't you? Well, let me tell you you're wrong!'

Fay at last began to understand this woman's jealousy.

'Good heavens, is *that* what you think? Then let me set your mind at rest,' she said firmly and clearly, looking her opponent straight in the eyes. 'I would not accept a post in *any* private maternity unit. I didn't train as a midwife just to kowtow to patients who can buy my co-operation—no way!'

'That's just sour grapes because you haven't been offered the post,' sneered Ann.

Fay thought of the number of times Lisle had tried to thrust the partnership upon her, but she checked herself from telling this hysterical woman; she had no wish to make them appear as rivals in love.

'Think what you like, Miss Clothier,' she said coldly. 'I'm proud to be a midwife for *all* women, not just those who can pay for VIP treatment. I *enjoy* working with the socially deprived, believe it or not—my poor young girls who never had a chance in life, housewives whose husbands are unemployed—ordinary women who have to make the best of their circumstances. The National Health Service may be far from perfect, but it's where I want to use my skills—it's my *choice*, if you can understand that. You're welcome to the Lisle Birthing Clinic, and good luck—with Lisle as the obstetrician, you're going to need it!'

Ann Clothier gasped and was about to retaliate when she caught sight of Dr Lewis Grant slowly descending the stairs behind Fay. There was a distinctly triumphant look on his face as he silently mouthed the word, Bravo. Fay was unaware of him, but to Ann he seemed to be watching over the girl and protecting her.

The senior midwife flashed Fay one last look of dislike, and withdrew to her office, slamming the door. Fay's heart was pounding as she hurried out into the freezing air, and she took several deep breaths to clear her head and restore her equilibrium. All she wanted was to get back to the flat after the upsets of the day, and she almost ran out of the main hospital entrance into Beltonshaw's main road.

And then she heard his voice close behind her.

'Fay.'

She spun round, hardly daring to believe that he had followed her.

'Fay, my love, are you all right? I heard that dreadful woman's outburst, and nearly cheered out loud at your reply! You mustn't let her upset you, you know.'

'Lewis! Oh, Lewis, never mind about *her*, she's to be pitied, poor thing,' responded Fay in confusion. 'All I'm worried about is the way I spoke to *you*.'

He caught her arm and held it tightly against his side as he fell into step beside her.

'Don't say a word about it, my love—it was *wonderful*! And it needed saying. My God, what a prize idiot I've been for so long, Fay! Will you ever be able to forgive me?'

All of a sudden the Beltonshaw main road seemed like a pathway to the stars. A great happiness began to well up inside Fay, and she could not answer him.

'I phoned home this evening, after I'd given that epidural,' he confided, smiling down at her. 'I spoke to my mother—and to Tommy.'

'Oh, Lewis, did you? What did he say?' she asked shyly.

'I told him that I'd met his friend Faith, and asked if he'd like me to bring her to see him again—soon.'

Fay could hardly breathe as she waited for him to go on.

'What about this Sunday, Fay?' His voice was low and full of tenderness.

'Why, yes, I—I've got a half-day then,' she managed to say, still wondering if she could really believe her ears.

'We could drive over as soon as you get off duty, then!'

'Together, Lewis?' He had to lean down to hear her faint whisper.

'Together, my darling.'

They stopped walking. She looked up into the familiar grey eyes, now alight with a love that had no need to hide a secret sorrow. And the cold, dark February night in a northern industrial suburb was transformed into the Garden of Eden. Passers-by smiled and a couple of youths cat-called as the two lovers kissed, standing on the icy pavement.

'Let's go to the flat and tell Susannah,' she whispered. 'Do you know about her and Matthew?'

He chuckled. 'I haven't officially been told anything, but I gather from the way he's walking on air and singing calypsos that the news is good!'

She laughed joyously. 'It's true, they're going to be married as soon as possible, and you and I are going to be witnesses. Isn't he wonderful, Lewis, taking on the responsibility for a child that isn't his own?'

'So are you, my little Fay, because you're doing just the same,' he reminded her as they linked arms again and walked on in a golden haze of happiness. Suddenly she looked up at him and said slyly,

'Excuse me, Dr Grant, but I don't think I actually heard you ask me to marry you—did I?'

'Ah, yes, that *is* a point,' he replied with deliberately grave formality. 'The fact is, Sister Mitchell, I don't think that Tommy will settle for anything less—do you?'

CHAPTER ELEVEN

SISTER MITCHELL'S patients and colleagues could not fail to notice the spring in her step and the look of jubilation in her dark brown eyes on Sunday morning, and at one o'clock she was ready to hand over the antenatal ward to Staff Nurse Laurie Moffatt, who came puffing up the stairs at the last minute.

'Sorry, Fay—I'm not late, am I? I've been out to lunch at a super restaurant in town!' she gasped.

'Get your breath back, Laurie, and I'll give you the report,' said Fay. 'Actually *I'm* going out to Sunday dinner, too, and want to get away.'

'Really?' asked the big blonde girl with interest. 'Aren't we both lucky! You'll never guess who took *me* out!'

'Now, let me see—could he possibly have been a newspaper photographer by the name of Roger?' asked Fay innocently.

'How did you know? So who's taking *you* out, then?' Fay lowered her eyes, and Laurie giggled. 'Ah, you think you can fool me, Sister Mitchell! It's not Nicholas Lisle, he's yesterday's man. No, your escort will be a certain anaesthetist with brooding eyes, by the name of——'

'Cut it out, Laurie, I want to get off duty!' protested Fay, blushing furiously.

'Quite right, we mustn't keep the gas-man waiting!'

The two girls laughed together, and gave each other a spontaneous hug.

Back at number thirty-seven Fay threw off her

179

uniform and put on a sturdy tweed skirt with a leather belt that emphasised her tiny waist. She chose a cream-coloured blouse in a soft wool and cotton mixture, with pleated frills at the neck and wrists, and pearl buttons down the front. Her light brown corduroy jacket was warm and windproof, and she decided to wear neat brown leather court shoes, slipping a pair of flat-heeled walking shoes into her capacious bag in case she and Lewis went walking in Barfylde. The general effect seemed to please her fiancé when he stood smiling up at her in admiration as she descended the stairs.

It was a cold, bright February afternoon, and Fay snuggled into her jacket as she sat beside Lewis in the car, watching the winter landscape unfold before them, with here and there a promise of spring: snowdrops nodding their brave heads, green shoots of early daffodils thrusting up through the frosty ground, and birds calling to each other in preparation for nesting time. Neither of them spoke much on the journey, and an unexpected shyness descended on Fay as she stole a glance at his profile; he was concentrating on driving fairly fast, especially when they were on the motorway. Her heart pounded as they covered the last few miles across country to Barfylde and Ively Lane, and she felt a little apprehensive as she walked through the door of Pear Tree Cottage. Only a few weeks ago she had come to this house as a stranger begging for shelter, and now she came as its future mistress, the intended wife of the owner. In the course of time she would become the mother of children who would grow up in this solid Victorian property: it would be her lifelong home, a centre of family life and a haven for friends.

There was no doubt about Tommy's ecstatic welcome and Fay held him tightly for a moment, closing her eyes; then she looked past him and saw his grandmother standing watching them, her bony features tense as she made an effort to adjust to the new circumstances. Mollie Grant knew that she was getting older, and was aware of failing strength; Tommy would be safely handed over to the care of this girl who had been sent into their lives, but Mollie felt sad at losing the guardianship of her beloved grandson.

Fay gently released the boy, and went to kiss her future mother-in-law.

'Hello, Mother.' They hugged each other, and Fay said softly, 'You won't ever regret asking me into your home.'

Mollie nodded, and began to scold herself briskly.

'Eh, lass, what am I thinking of? Here's you and Lewis, fair starving after your journey, and me hanging around like a spare part when I should be dishing up t' dinner!'

When all four of them were seated at the kitchen table, the atmosphere relaxed considerably.

'When are you coming to live with us, Faith?' asked Tommy excitedly.

Fay glanced shyly at his father. They had already decided on a four-month engagement.

'We'll have to wait for a little while yet,' smiled Lewis. 'There are going to be a lot of changes! I need to get settled in my new job with the group practice at Kirkby Lonsdale, and I'll be living here at home after the first of March. We're going to have some renovations done on this house before I bring my wife into it, so we think that a June wedding would be just about right!'

'Yes, and I have to look for work in this area,' added Fay, noting the way Mollie's face brightened as she realised that the handing over of the household would be a gradual process.

'How would you feel about being a practice nurse attached to a GP group, darling?' asked Lewis with sudden inspiration. 'My future colleagues are talking of appointing one to keep up with the trend!'

'*Lewis*! Do you think they'd have me?' asked Fay eagerly. 'I can't think of anything I'd like more than working alongside you in a group practice. Does yours hold an antenatal clinic?'

'Of course! The usual shared care with the hospital. There's also a special women's clinic for family planning, cervical smears, blood-pressure checks and so on,' continued Lewis, 'to say nothing of child welfare and immunisation programmes. And at the other end of the scale we have a retirement clinic where we do check-ups and offer influenza jabs—it's a very wide-ranging field, Fay, if you think you'd enjoy it.'

'*Would* I? Here I am, if the practice wants to take me on!' she told him, her dark eyes sparkling.

When dinner had been cleared away, Mollie Grant very firmly announced that she and Tommy were going for a walk down to the village.

'Sister Concilia is laid up with arthritis at t' convent, and I've got a dozen new-laid eggs for her,' she explained.

'Oh, *no*, Granny, not while Faith and Daddy are here!' wailed Tommy.

'Hush, lad, you know Sister needs cheering up, and besides, we must let Daddy have some time to himself with our Faith,' replied his grandmother, busily doing up her coat buttons and tying on a headscarf. 'Right, Lewis, we'll be out for a full hour!'

And, taking Tommy by the hand, she marched out into the winter sunshine.

'Oh, Lewis, there was no need for her to——' began Fay.

'It's all right, darling, my mother wants to show us that she understands,' he reassured her, pulling her towards him as they stood in the warm kitchen. 'We should accept our hour with thanks! Oh, I can't tell you what it means to see you here at home, dearest Fay. . .'

He folded her close and kissed the top of the dark curly head that nestled against his chest. 'I want to share it all with you, and talk about some of the alterations I've got in mind for the place.'

Fay felt that she did not want to alter a thing, and a few minutes later, when he led her into the main bedroom, she felt like an intruder. Mollie still slept in the carved oak bed she had shared with her husband, and the massive wardrobes and dressing-table stood exactly as they had done for over forty years.

'Mother will be moving out of here into my room,' he said. 'This will be ours.'

Fay could not meet hs eyes, but locked her arms around his middle.

'It needs completely redecorating in much lighter colours—say cream and rose, with a nice thick carpet for you to walk on in your bare feet!' he told her with boyish enthusiasm. 'All this furniture will be replaced by a built-in suite. What sort of a bed would you like, darling?'

'Oh, I like *this* one!' she said at once. 'I mean if your mother wouldn't mind—oak's a lovely wood, and I've always wanted to sleep in a great big bed with——'

He laughed delightedly as he took her into his arms again, and this time she thrilled to the very core of her being at the touch of those strong, masterful hands that she had so often seen at work, bringing relief from pain and expertly reviving the newly born. Now she felt them gently cupping the soft roundness of her breasts, and sweeping over her narrow hips: she was aware of Lewis as an eager lover, and his closeness, his warmth and his sudden urgent need for possession of her overcame all her reservations.

She put her arms around his neck and opened her mouth for his kisses. Her eyes closed in a swooning wave of joyful anticipation, and her body seemed to melt as she felt his lips upon her mouth, her cheeks, her eyes, her ears, even a butterfly touch on the tip of her nose. . .

And then the creamy blouse was opening as his fingers gently but determinedly began to undo the buttons, revealing her neck and shoulders to his questing mouth. She felt his hands passing under the soft material to her back, and unhooking her lace-trimmed bra.

'Yes, Lewis—oh, yes!' she murmured, surrendering to the unbelievable sensation of his mouth upon her breasts.

'Fay, my little, little Fay, I love you so much,' he whispered, and, straightening himself up for a moment, he took off his tie and flung aside the knitted pullover he had been wearing over a white shirt. Fay began to unfasten his shirt buttons, but her fingers were shaking so much that he gently closed one strong, warm hand over hers and quickly released the shirt with his other hand.

And then they were clasped together, his bared chest against her curving flesh.

'I've loved you, Fay, I've loved you from the beginning, right from the very moment I first saw you in Maternity,' he told her between kisses.

'I think I've loved you, too, Lewis, without knowing it,' she confided, 'but I was certain at Christmas, after

Rachel Bamford's baby was born, and we were in the office——'

'Under the mistletoe, yes,' he remembered, holding her close.

'Lewis, this is still your mother's bed. Take me to *your* room,' she said in a low voice, and at once he led her by the hand to the room where she had slept on New Year's Eve.

With one firm, sweeping movement he picked her up, just as 'Batman' had done, and laid her upon his bed. She still had her skirt on, he still wore his belted trousers, and made no move to discard them when he covered her body with his own, crushing her down into the bed. Her arms were around him and her hands caressed his back, running her fingers down his spine. It was such a strong, muscular back, with smooth, unblemished skin, and Fay was overwhelmed by this excitingly unfamiliar Lewis. She revelled in the sheer sensuality of the weight of his body upon hers. Her eyes clouded with desire for complete fulfilment of their love, and she begged him breathlessly, urgently.

'Love me, Lewis! Love me now! Ah, Lewis. . .'

He gave a sigh that was almost a groan.

'God knows I want you, Fay, but—*no*! Not yet,' he muttered incoherently, and with a superhuman effort he turned over so that he was lying beside her. 'Darling, I mustn't. You mustn't let me. I love you too much, Fay—oh, my God——' He broke off and put his hand over his face for an instant. Fay sat up.

'Lewis, dear, what on earth's the matter?'

'Fay—you know I got a girl pregnant once before— it mustn't happen to you, darling. Please forgive me, it's not because I don't want——'

She put a finger upon his lips.

'Shh, Lewis, it's all right. I understand. Don't say any more.'

And for a few minutes they lay side by side, hands clasped, looking searchingly into each other's faces. Fay was aware that even now she still had the power to persuade him, to tempt and seduce him into complete union with her, but she did not want him to have regrets. It was not only because of his past. The nature of her work as a midwife also had a restraining effect: they daily saw so much sadness and disillusionment. She thought of Susannah. Lewis and she were different, but. . .

'How I shall make love to you when we're in the big bed together!' he promised with a look that made her spine tingle, though she wagged an admonishing finger at him as she got up from the bed.

'I'm going to make some tea,' she said. 'Mother and Tommy will be home soon, and——'

He leaned over and tightened his hold on her for a moment.

'One more thing, dearest Fay—have I to call you Faith now, like Tommy?'

'I'll answer to both,' she smiled, and they kissed deeply once more before hastily putting on their top clothes and descending the stairs hand in hand, shaken by the storm of passion that had so quickly engulfed them. Both were thinking that it was perhaps as well that there would be few opportunities to be alone during their engagement.

And both regretted that June was so far away from February.

If friends and colleagues were disappointed at the discreetly quiet wedding of Dr Okoje and Sister Starr, they were more than compensated by the joyful celebrations that took place when Dr Grant married Sister Mitchell at the Beltonshaw church of St Antony's on a brilliant Saturday in early June.

Long before the bride arrived the church was full of eager whispers of anticipaton. Sister Pardoe was seated next to Mr and Mrs Horsfield, in front of the Rowans; and across the aisle from them was the radiant Mrs Okoje with her devoted friend Mrs Abigail Leroy, who insisted on holding three-week-old Lucy during the service so that Susannah could give her full attention to it.

On the bride's side in the front pew sat a curly-haired young man whose mischievous eyes caught the attention of the student midwives as he sat beside his stepmother; his resemblance to his sister identified him as Able-Seaman Roy Mitchell, and he amused the company by giving a broad wink of encouragement across the aisle to his future brother-in-law who sat nervously beside the best man, Dr Okoje. Further along the pew Mollie Grant looked equally tense, and was glad of the support of her niece Jenny who had brought her two little girls to the wedding.

Nudges were exchanged and heads craned to see the arrival of Joanna Leach and her husband, accompanied by Roger the photographer, who waved and blew a kiss to a smiling Laurie Moffatt.

There were a couple of absentees from this happy gathering. Dr Lisle had found that the conversion of his newly acquired property into the Lisle Birthing Clinic was taking up so much of his time that he was unable to attend the wedding of that silly girl who had thrown away a great future; and Miss Clothier had decided to leave Beltonshaw General Hospital when she realised that she was not going to be offered a clinic post with Dr Lisle.

The organ began to peal out the 'Bridal March', and all eyes turned to the back of the church as the congregation rose, and Father Naylor took his place in front of the altar. Sighs of admiration greeted the first appearance of the bride in a heavenly white lace dress. She proceeded slowly up the aisle on her father's arm, followed by two attendants who walked hand in hand. Dr Rose Gillis, in a pale blue dress and her long black hair hanging loose from a centre-parting, made an enchanting bridesmaid; but a flurry of questions rippled across the congregation at the sight of the bright-eyed boy beside her, dressed in a neat navy suit with bow-tie. He drew smiles from everybody, and his slightly limping gait was scarcely noticed. The grey-haired lady in the front pew turned and gazed intently at the boy, her gaunt features illumined with pride and satisfaction. Whispers flew back and forth.

'He must be Dr Grant's son!'

'The lad's the image of his dad!'

'Doesn't Fay look gorgeous?'

'What about the bridegroom? He's staring at her like a man bewitched!'

Lewis Grant felt that all he had ever hoped or dreamed of had come true on this wonderful day. As his grey eyes held the gaze of the exquisite little bride now walking towards him, he knew that the sorrow of the past was over, like the winter left behind and forgotten in the summer sunshine.

Fay knew very well that the new life now beginning would not be free from problems, and that their profession would continue to involve both of them with sad situations in the lives of others. But she also knew that the love they shared would shine out in kindness and compassion to all around them, a bright light in the community and a warm glow in their home.

PRESENT
THE 50TH ROMANCE BY
JESSICA STEELE
'DESTINED TO MEET'

Popular Romance author Jessica Steele finds her inspiration by travelling extensively and researching her backgrounds. But she hates to leave her delightfully soppy Staffordshire Bull Terrier, Daisy, behind, and likes nothing better than to work in her study overlooking a beautiful Worcestershire valley, backed by a hill and a long stretch of trees – "an ideal spot for writing" she says.

You're sure to agree when you read her latest intriguing love story *'Destined to Meet'* – don't miss it!

Published: October 1992   Price: £1.70

BARBARY WHARF
BOOK 5

Now that Gib and Valerie have found each other, what is to become of Guy Faulkner, the *Sentinel* lawyer, and Sophie Watson his secretary, both rejected and abandoned by the people they loved.

Could they find solace together, or was Sophie at least determined not to fall in love on the rebound, even if Guy did seem to think it was time for him to find true love?

Find out in Book 5 of Barbary Wharf —

A SWEET ADDICTION

Available: September 1992   Price: £2.99

W❂RLDWIDE